THE TRUMAN QUEST

D S Bruce

Matador
Unit E2 Airfield Business Park,
Harrison Road, Market Harborough,
Leicestershire. LE16 7UL
Tel: 0116 2792299
Email: books@troubador.co.uk
Web: www.troubador.co.uk/matador
Twitter: @matadorbooks

ISBN 978 1803132 150

British Library Cataloguing in Publication Data.
A catalogue record for this book is available from the British Library.

Printed and bound by CPI Group (UK) Ltd, Croydon, CR0 4YY
Type

For Sue, who made it possible
And for Dan, Alex, Charlotte, Richard,
Ada and Ethan

ONE

Fifteen-year-old Ray Bradnock loved that sign on the office door, with its promise of excitement and insight into the mysterious world of adults. He'd been regularly visiting his Uncle Garry's place of work since the start of his Easter holidays, and had yet to discover either excitement, insight, or even much evidence of work. Still, he held on to the prospect of adventure with something of a frantic grip because he desperately needed some sense of hope and purpose.

His mother and father had separated six months ago in Birmingham and, to be honest, amongst the chaotic blame-shouting of splitting parents, it hadn't felt like either of them was overly bothered about who got custody. He'd finished up at the seaside in Devon with his mother, where he was slowly drowning in self-loathing. Nobody seemed remotely interested in swimming out and saving him. His mother simply told him to paddle harder. His Uncle Garry, at least, let him hang around his office.

But today, the office door was already open as he and his uncle arrived back from a 'missing person' case, and Gerald Dunstable, the leading light of Brookdale-on-Sea, was sitting in Leary's chair, his grey suit-jacket unfastened, looking cool, pleasant and collected. Charlie Manley, a short, stout businessman with a reputation for ruthlessness, and owner of the local fairground, was standing behind him on his right. Ray recognised the tall, moustachioed Jonas Warrington from their meeting the previous day. He was his uncle's rival in the world of private investigation and stood looking uncomfortable on Dunstable's left.

Leary was puzzled, but before he had the chance to speak Dunstable leaned across the desk, smiled and held out his hand.

'Good afternoon, Mr Leary. I don't think we've had the pleasure. This is Mr Charles Manley, and Warrington here I think you already know. Do, please, sit down.'

Leary, releasing the hand offered him, sat down slowly, the puzzled expression deepening on his face. Ray stood uncertainly behind him.

'I wonder if you would excuse us, young man,' Dunstable said, looking pleasantly at him.

Leary roused himself. 'Hang on! This is my place, so I decide who goes and stays.'

'Really? Technically, that's not quite true though, is it, Mr Leary? You rent your premises and I happen to be its landlord. I also own your current accommodation in... Albert Street, is it?' He looked to Warrington, who barely nodded, before continuing. 'The Dunstables really do have a great deal of property in the town.

'Look, I've been rather remiss in not introducing myself formally. I'm Gerald Dunstable, co-founder and chair of Vader International. I'm sure you've heard of it – the new technology company I'm starting up that's about to revolutionise Silicon Valley from right here in sunny Devon! I'm also chair of the Chamber of Trade, chair of the Charities' Guild and chair of the Churches' Council. And, of course, chair of the Local Economy and Enterprise Board.'

Leary looked steadily into the handsome, tanned, smiling face opposite him. He knew the type: genial, smug and with the enormous confidence inherited privilege brought them.

'Sounds knackering, but it keeps you off the streets, don't it?' Leary observed pleasantly. 'And you can always take the weight off your feet by sitting on all them chairs.'

Dunstable frowned momentarily. Unfortunately, Leary was definitely one of those bumptious, working-class oiks he avoided at all costs. He was pleased he had brought the other two men along.

He smiled and continued as pleasantly as before. 'Yes... Well, we have something in common, I believe, Mr Leary. I think my father was in the Devonshire Light Infantry Regiment at the same time you were actually.'

'Right... That'd be "Dumpy" Dunstable, would it?' Leary commented. 'Tubby little lance corporal with a squint and flatulence. Yeah, if your old dad bent over sudden, like, he could blow a wig off at fifty paces. Always a right scramble not sharing a pup tent with him.'

'No, Mr Leary,' Dunstable explained patiently, 'I'm speaking of Brigadier General Sir Robert Dunstable, KCB. He was your regimental commanding officer at the time.'

'Nah. Not the same feller at all then. Dumpy was strictly a KFC man. A Big Mac brought out the flatulence something rotten.'

'I told you it'd be a waste of time talking to this—' began Manley but stopped as Dunstable raised his hand.

'You got him well house-trained,' Leary observed admiringly as Manley's pink face deepened to red. 'Standing there like that, he knows he ain't allowed up on the furniture.'

'Ignore it, Charles, please,' Dunstable counselled, before turning his attention again to Leary.

'You know, Mr Leary, you're relatively new to the town. I've come here, in neighbourly fashion—'

'All three of you,' Leary interjected.

Dunstable continued, as if he hadn't heard, '… simply to try and bring certain matters of… protocol to your attention. We all have our places in society, don't we?'

'That what you reckon, is it? See, my problem is I don't know mine. Never have. All that touching-your-forelock-to-your-betters stuff you just served up, don't really do it for me, Mr Dunstable. I mean, when you crack one off, I bet it ain't exactly Chanel No. 5, is it?'

'Look, shall we try and keep the conversation pleasant and civilised to avoid embarrassing the boy? You obviously don't appreciate, Mr Leary, that I'm working pretty well tirelessly to promote the best interests of this town.'

Leary looked to Warrington. 'Ahhh, that's nice, eh, Jonas, Mother Teresa in a suit there. Any chance of a few quid in it for you?' he asked Dunstable.

'Do you know, I'm finding your attempts at levity just a trifle wearisome and that last insinuation, actually, rather offensive,' Dunstable observed, his face deadly serious.

'Not much of a sense of humour, has he, Jonas? Old Dumpy Junior there.' Leary directed Warrington's attention to the younger man with a nod.

'Listen, Leary,' Manley cut in, 'I know some wasteland out of town where we can sort this out if you prefer.'

'That an invitation to your fairground, Charlie, the one with a booth for the Samaritans?'

'Listen, you!' Manley said, starting around the desk.

Dunstable closed his eyes and shook his head. He was losing control of the situation. The little oik was certainly annoying and no push-over.

'Charles. Let me handle this. Please.'

Manley, breathing heavily, stopped. 'He'd better watch hisself!' he spat out.

'Just let it go, Charles. We really don't want an incident. You understand?'

'Is that one woof for yes and two for no, "Charles"?' Leary asked, smiling.

Dunstable raised his eyebrows to Ray as if pitying him for the embarrassment his uncle was causing. 'You know, Mr Leary, we're all trying very hard to be patient with you. You have absolutely no idea what you're stumbling into the middle of.'

'Yeah… Well, I'm guessing it don't smell too good, Mr Dunstable, or you wouldn't have brought along Rover and Fido there,' Leary said, nodding at the two men opposite. 'Now, what exactly is it you want?'

'You're currently involved in a missing person case,' Dunstable stated, examining and twizzling a diamond ring round his little finger, before looking up. 'A Mr Truman, isn't it?'

'Cheers, Jonas. So much for the "professional courtesy", eh?' Leary said contemptuously to Warrington, who lowered his gaze to the floor. 'Might be… What about it?'

'Well, I'd rather like you to drop it.'

'Say again?' Leary asked, leaning forward.

'I said, I'd like you to drop the case. You see, this is a delicate, somewhat complicated affair and it's already being investigated by Warrington here.'

'That so? Well, I can't really do that, as Warrington here, the "professional", will confirm, on account of there being a thing known as "contractual obligations" to the client. Sort of a matter of principle, see.'

'Do you know, that's really amusing, Leary, because you don't look to me like the kind of man who can actually afford principles. You're wearing a cheap suit in even cheaper surroundings. Not exactly the Taj Mahal here, is it?'

His nostrils flared as he sniffed, looking around a room that had, in Ray's view, achieved a level of 'tat' that verged on genius. A dying houseplant on a dented, green filing cabinet presided over second-hand furniture and a sticky brown carpet. Leary's dedication to getting the very last drop of nicotine from his roll-up cigarettes had decorated the ceiling a drab yellow. The office, smelling of stale smoke and damp, reminded Ray of all the elegance and warmth to be found in bus station waiting rooms.

'Blame it on the landlord, eh?' Leary suggested, winking.

'Oh, how scintillatingly witty!' Dunstable smiled sardonically. 'On the other hand, you're hardly Gianni Versace when it comes to interior design, are you? To be brutally frank, this dump looks like it was thrown together by a blind man with no sense of smell or taste.'

'Yeah, well you may be into boudoirs and perfume, Brutal Frank, but I ain't. Suits me as it is, ta. Anything else before you go?'

'Yes. Drop the case. You see, the consequences are going to be very serious if you don't. We have the genesis of what is looking like a world-dominating technology company right here in Brookdale. And I have absolutely no intention of allowing someone of your sort to jeopardise important developments for this town, or indeed, the country at large.'

'"My sort"?' Leary challenged.

Dunstable smiled. 'Well, I would really rather not have had to say this in front of the boy there, but... since you seem to pride yourself on "straight talking"... What I mean is, I have no intention of allowing a sleazy, third-rate little turd like you to gum up the works.'

'Listen—' began Leary, the colour coming to his face, but Dunstable spoke over him.

'No. No, I really, really do insist that *you* listen, Leary. You see, we've been poking around into your squalid little history. A disinfectant scrub after the experience would have been very welcome, because frankly, old man, your life really does reek almost as bad as this place does.'

He took out a notebook and began reading from it. 'Fascinating childhood and adolescence. Numerous run-ins with the law... Cautions for handling stolen goods... Cautions for wilful damage to property. Um, two cautions for alcohol and drug abuse. A suspended juvenile sentence for drunk and disorderly behaviour. Early expulsion from school. How very, very distinguished! A real little Churchill!

'Because then, just like dear old Winston and his mediocre school performance, a military career beckoned, apparently. Ten or so odd years of disciplinary infractions and then you finally managed to hit the jackpot! Two years in an army detention centre for fraud and conduct unbecoming of a member of Her Majesty's Forces Overseas.'

Dunstable snapped the book closed and leaned back in the chair.

'Look, I've no wish to be here any longer than I need, so let's just summarise, shall we? You're basically an ex-convict, Leary, forty-two years old and drifting from one dead-end job to the next, with no money, home, family or prospects. Do you know, if you had any friends at all I'd be mightily surprised now I've met you? All this... brashness masking disappointment with a crummy little life. You're not exactly the best role model for the boy there, are you – felon, gambler and regular drunk?'

Dunstable spoke with the calm, measured sense of superiority borne of 200 years of the best breeding. 'I can have you out of this... dump, unable to practise your sordid little trade within a hundred-mile radius. And all before you could say "loser". And that, Leary, is precisely what you are: a lonely loser with a sizeable chip on his shoulder, masquerading as company. I mean, really, who else but a loser would operate from a "stink hole" like this?'

He gestured around the office, before continuing. 'Tell me, would you like me to regale the boy here with some further unsavoury morsels from "The Leary Hall of Fame"?'

Leary looked down at his hands, Warrington shifted uncomfortably, while Manley smiled broadly.

'No? Somehow, I thought not... So, finally, we appear to be understanding each other,' Dunstable said after a long pause.

He stood up slowly, a tall man accustomed to looking down on others, and fastened his jacket with elegant ease. Reaching into his pocket he dropped a brown envelope into Leary's lap.

'Two hundred pounds in there to cover whatever expenses you've incurred. And I suppose you could lose the rest on a little flutter at the bookies and getting soused.'

He paused and Leary remained looking down where the envelope had landed.

'That's quite an impression you must have made on your nephew today! Sort of a chip off the old block,' Dunstable observed.

As he was about to pass out of the door, Leary turned in his seat and called out, 'Mr Dunstable!'

Dunstable stopped and turned in the doorway.

'You're dead right. I been bang out of order. I didn't recognise you to start with, but you're definitely a chip off the old block an' all. Spitting image of your old dad,' Leary observed, nodding and smiling.

He paused, whilst Dunstable looked magnanimously at him, before adding, 'He was a stuck-up, toffee-arsed ponce an' all.'

He skimmed the envelope back at Dunstable who caught it deftly. For a moment he contemplated Leary who was looking down again at his lap. Then, slowly returning the money to his inside jacket pocket, he spoke with ice-cool precision, the fixed smile back on his lips, and looking even deadlier.

'Oh dear. That's likely to be a very, very costly error of judgement, Leary.'

He turned and walked out of the room.

'I'm having you, Leary. Personally!' Manley hissed, pointing a stubby finger at him.

'Tell me, "Charles", do you ever just throw all dignity to the wind, roll over and let him tickle your belly?' Leary asked wearily.

Manley gave a contemptuous laugh. 'It's a frickin' miracle!' he said to Warrington. 'A dead man talking. Come on.'

He followed Dunstable out of the room. Jonas Warrington, walking with his eyes fixed on the ground, paused next to Leary as if to speak.

'Here! Jonas!' Manley shouted from down the corridor.

'Dog's life, ain't it?' Leary observed to Warrington. 'Mind you don't widdle on the stairs on your way out.'

Warrington's face clouded, he changed his mind and left.

A stillness settled on the room that seemed to Ray to last a long, long time. Finally, his uncle got up and moved over to the filing cabinet, his back to his nephew. He rattled open the bottom drawer and took out its only contents: a bottle of whisky and a tumbler.

'Are you okay?' Ray asked apprehensively.

Ray could see his hand trembling as he leaned against the cabinet and poured himself a very large Scotch.

He stood facing the wall, gulped down the contents and said, in a strangely lifeless voice without turning, 'Get yourself home now, boy.'

Ray was about to speak again, thought better of it and went out, closing the door behind him.

TWO

B ack home, Ray lay on his bed, an 'activity' he was doing an awful lot of recently. His games console had been temporarily confiscated due to his last school report. Apparently, he was 'Below Average' in every subject on the curriculum, apart from the woodwork element of Design Technology, and Religious Education, where he was 'Average'. Mr Williams, the woodwork man, appreciated his enthusiasm, even if he didn't always admire his handiwork. Mrs Noble, the RE lady, hadn't got the slightest clue who Ray Bradnock was.

Dad, a trained carpenter, had attempted on occasions in the past to instil a feel for the qualities of the medium – wood – but had always abandoned the enterprises as Ray's clumsiness escalated his frustration from dead-eyed, forced smile to pop-out-eyed fury.

The last ever lesson (though, sadly, Ray didn't realise it at the time) on the correct use of the 'plane' in the cold, dank shed, had been painfully memorable, with Ray starting blank-faced, wondering what aircraft had to do with joinery, until his father had taken the heavy tool down from its carefully allotted position on the shelf.

By the time Ray had followed the detailed instructions, adjusted his feet and legs to the 'correct angle', his body at an inclination that would deliver maximum heft, and his hands with the palms this way, and the fingers that way and the thumbs whatever way, he could no more have planed a centimetre off a door's bottom than he could have sculpted the Venus de Milo's.

'No, son, hold it like this and push through from the shoulders,' Mr Bradnock had instructed, pushing and pulling Ray's various body parts into convoluted positions. 'Come on... Come on! Push through from the centre of your frame!' Mr Bradnock demanded, while Ray's eyes grew glassy and distant, and his body lost all connection with his brain.

His father had the patience of a man already late for an appointment, stuck behind a tractor, and Ray's lumbering ineptitude bulked out exponentially under his critical scrutiny. Actually, Ray didn't care for woodwork. He just wanted to feel loved and a 'real man'.

A mediocre career carving crucifixes seemed to beckon, according to his report and father's sarcastic, 'witty' observation on the phone, and if Ray didn't 'pull his finger out' (though he didn't specify out of what), he'd be joining that long line of deadbeats queuing for benefits.

Lying there, Ray felt distinctly queasy as he reviewed the last two days' events. He'd seen plenty of kids, but never a grown-up, bullied and humiliated. He'd also had no previous notion of his uncle's 'squalid' past. He felt ashamed both for, and of, the man. On top of that he felt ashamed for feeling ashamed!

Closing his eyes only brought replay after replay of the repulsive but fascinating scene, because that 'lonely loser' jibe from Mr Dunstable had seemed to ricochet off his uncle and headed straight, whack, into Ray's psyche! Except that it hadn't ricocheted off because Ray had seen the effects on him after the others had left. To see a grown-up degraded reinforced the feeling that Ray was always, somehow, going to find life too brutal and scary, whatever age he became.

*

It had all started on Monday, the previous day, when Ray had been visiting his uncle and found him in his usual position: chair tilted, head in the *Racing Post* and feet nestling amongst ashtrays, mugs and papers scattered across his desk.

'Alright,' Leary had yawned, circling 'Mucky Man' for the two-fifteen Doncaster race. 'You got a quid for the meter?'

Visiting Uncle Garry was proving to be an expensive hobby for his nephew.

'Ta. Stick it in the gaffins then… How's Mum?' Leary asked, his bloodshot eyes focusing on the three o'clock at Haydock.

'Good, yeah. I was—'

'Here. Get us a brew, will you? Need to clear me head a bit. Pronto, eh, son.'

Since this was the best conversation Ray was likely to get all day, he'd set about making the coffees. He would have really welcomed an opportunity to gab about gorgeous classmate Susannah Payne, who wasn't aware and didn't care if he existed. Or popular sports captain Leon Rogers, who cared enough to call him 'Brummie Brasscock', whilst playfully and sadistically slapping his head in corridors.

He hadn't shared any of this with Leary because he really didn't know a whole lot about the man; just what he'd earwigged from past, murmured conversations between his parents. He gathered he was something of an awkward, bad lot. He'd shifted from Hackney to the town of Brookdale-on-Sea soon after their arrival.

He definitely possessed a certain lizard-like fascination. Physically he was slight in build and under average height. He had had to scrap as a youngster to gain the respect the bigger boys were automatically accorded. He lost many a fight, but no one had ever defeated him. He got up again to face opponents no matter how many times they flattened him. Most walked away, shaking their heads in bewilderment and muttering 'headcase', as Leary staggered to his feet demanding further satisfaction.

His face, though somewhat coarse in features, was arresting: the eyes a stark blue, the skin tanned and weather-beaten with a scar on the chin, and the black hair thinning and slicked back over the skull. A former soldier, he carried his natty, and occasionally crumpled, wardrobe of flash suits and bilious ties with a certain style and panache. His complexion and the beginning of a broadening around his middle suggested that alcohol was an old, much entertained friend.

What fascinated Ray most about him were his observations on life – so different from anyone else's. Ray's upbringing had been utterly, boringly conventional. He'd been taught to respect his elders and 'betters', to know his place and present a cheerful, grateful front to them all. Leary, on the other hand, considered his 'betters' as having gained their advantages through sneaky, convoluted shenanigans, had no time for deference and flaunted his dismissal of them at any opportunity.

'Them charmers at the top, they'll kick you in the teeth every time, 'cos they've already decided there ain't room for anybody else up there,' was a philosophy he embraced and occasionally preached.

If there was such a thing as a 'Grand Order to the Universe', Garry Anthony Leary was probably the inaccessible bit at the bottom, back, left-hand corner, which could drip dark, corrosive fluid and wouldn't be reached without a special spanner. A man who had seen a lot of life and viewed it with contempt and amusement was intriguing, but also a little scary to his nephew.

He lay down his paper with a weary sigh and looked at his watch. 'I got a punter here in five minutes. Name of…'

He sifted through the top layer of desk debris and picked out a yellow post-it.

'Truman. Zita Truman… Zita, eh? Sounds exotic. Here! Tidy that lot up for us, will you, boy?'

Ray cleared the desk while his uncle pulled up his tie and checked his appearance in the chrome side of the broken water boiler.

'Nip down to the bookies. You know Jack Sunderland. Ask him to lay that lot on for us. Pronto, son!'

He passed Ray a £20 note and a yellow post-it with racehorse names on it, as a timid knock sounded at the door. He jerked his head at it to indicate the lad should leave. As Ray opened the door a tall, middle-aged woman with glasses, lank, grey hair under a red beret and pulling a shopping trolley stepped in. She nodded to Ray. He nodded back before closing the door and sighing.

The exotic Zita looked like she had all the glamour and mystery of a three-day-old pizza.

Having delivered the bet to Mr Sunderland, Ray had headed down to the seafront. Brookdale was certainly a treat of a place after Birmingham – glittering sea, great coastline and cafes and amusements to while away the time. Problem was if you didn't have any mates to share it with, you looked even more peculiar walking round on your tod. Ray had always felt something of a loner, never through choice, and he hated it! He'd struggled to fit in at infant and junior schools, and secondary education often felt little less than a daily nightmare. The recent move had further increased his sense of anxious detachment from the 'Cool Kids' Club' – wherever or whatever that was.

Added to that was the fact that he had recently lost yet another phone. This was the third one he'd broken or lost in eighteen months. His mother had been less than impressed and much of his paper-round money was being put aside to supplement the cost of a cheap replacement. Of course, that put him well out of the loop of social media, which, as far as Ray was concerned, was just fine and dandy!

Because, honestly, was there anything more dispiriting than sitting by yourself, scrolling down screen after screen of people sounding upbeat and delighted to be communicating with each other? With your own cautious attempt to break into the social merry-go-round being greeted with a couple of minutes of enigmatic blankness, before participants felt sufficient time had elapsed to pass over the embarrassment and resume the camaraderie.

Or was that just being totally paranoid? There was certainly no better way to increase that feeling than going on a social site! His temporary exile from social media and his own lack of concern, if not positive relief about it, were also a real cause of worry for his mother. The general theme was that he should be making more of an effort to mix with his peers and to make some 'proper' friends, because it certainly wasn't 'normal' hanging round with someone like his uncle.

If Ray was honest, he already considered himself something of a 'weirdo', so Mother's subtle reinforcement of that feeling was hardly helpful. He had seemed condemned to struggle with that feeling of being 'different', but not in a good way, since from when he could remember. He had never, ever felt comfortable in his own skin, sensing there was something basically 'just not right' about himself. He couldn't get a handle on what it was. Whatever it was didn't seem to actively repel people. It just didn't seem to attract that many.

The prospect of ambling nonchalantly up to a group of classmates, casually chatting amongst themselves and usually joshing one of the congregation, felt as threatening in the pit of your stomach as shinning down a tall, slippery sycamore. And, if you opened up with the suicidal gambit, 'I'm lonely, will you be my friends?', you might as well go all out, drop your trousers and stencil 'Oddball' on your forehead!

How stupid was that! And yet the fear was genuine because you never knew if they would welcome, ignore or select you as the butt, beating your soul with sarcasm and amiable contempt. Having to stand there, semi-paralysed, with a rictus grin on your face, as people 'playfully' ridiculed your features, name, clothing or character was the one place you never wanted to be.

'Banter'. That was what the clever people used to humiliate you; insults with a laugh thrown in at the end to camouflage the sadism. And you never had the time or speed of mind to be able to swing one back, with a sharp, snidey 'haymaker' that lifted their nastiness clean off the ground and laid it out cold.

He had had one moment of reassurance at the new school. Hanging around the corner of the old ROSLA block, unseen at lunchtime, he'd overheard a conversation between two girls he'd always considered cool and somewhat aloof. The coolest of the pair was quietly crying, and Ray had been amazed and temporarily comforted that, at least, one other person also detested the place and the 'cows' there giving her a hard time. Unfortunately, the comforting sense of identifying with her struggles had been only temporary, dissipating when she'd appeared to ignore his nod of greeting in form group at afternoon registration.

If school days really were the happiest time of your life, a sentiment his parents had insisted to be the case whenever they felt he needed to 'buck up his ideas and get on with it', then, jeez, what was the rest of it going to look like?!

Uncle Garry had a very different take on schooling, or 'open chokey' as he called it. By the time they finished washing and scrubbing out the old brain, he reckoned, most people hadn't got a single, solitary, original idea left in their bonces. You not only didn't get time off for good behaviour in this particular prison, but the better you behaved, the longer they insisted you stayed put!

Leary could calculate, almost to a decimal point, how keen to conclude his school career his own teachers had been. He had left to a chorus of sighs of relief and confident predictions that he would never amount to anything but trouble. The oddest part, Ray thought, being that his uncle was more than happy with the prediction.

'I mean, for crying out loud, boy, who wants some deadbeat teacher, finally managing to be the biggest, hardest kid in the class, giving their miserable, bleedin' blessing?'

Reaching the promenade, Ray plonked himself down on the nearest vacant bench. Behind him a large sign was being craned up into place above a block of what had previously been residential flats.

'VADER INTERNATIONAL', it proclaimed in three-foot-high, purple letters.

Here were the headquarters of the new technology company that was already employing a hundred or so of Brookdale-on-Sea's residents, Ray's mother amongst them. It was the biggest thing ever to have hit the place, with a factory nearing completion on the outskirts.

Up in the penthouse suite of Vader International, the genius inventor behind the company lay glowing, face down under the blue rays of a sunbed. Heavy-metal music was pounding out tinnily from the headphones dangling from his hand. Beside him, Gerald Dunstable, handsome and aristocratic, looked down with distaste at the prodigy's bare, mottled back.

'And, Gerald, get that moron to follow the specifications accurately, will you?' the figure on the bed murmured lazily.

Dunstable marvelled again at the mind of a creature who could dismiss the acknowledged and admired expert in his field as a 'moron'.

'Ian,' Dunstable said quietly, 'you really will have to bear with him. Stapleton's the best there is. Actually, I think the poor man's pretty close to cracking up.'

His boss mumbled some dismissive comment and waved him away.

'We'll be needing the blueprints for the final stage,' Dunstable coaxed gently. 'We're almost three weeks behind schedule and the investors are asking... rather awkward questions.

'You know, Ian, they've never been exactly delighted with our choice of location. "The back end of nowhere", one of them called it yesterday. They all favoured that site in Kent. So, we really will have to work at keeping them on side. Come on, Ian, let's try and hit that deadline and go for it!'

An annoyed grunt was the only response. Dunstable recognised the interview was over and made for the lift.

'And get them to hurry up with that stupid sign, will you!' Vader called out petulantly. 'I'm getting a really bad head again! You should be taking better care of me, Gerald, and sorting out the other!'

He replaced the headphones and let his forehead settle back on the sunbed.

Dunstable was furious. He hadn't wanted the damned sign or location in the first place! The site in Kent would have been less than a half-hour helicopter ride to the centre of London, his favoured destination for living the sophisticated lifestyle he considered worthy of his station. It was Vader, in a rare intervention into the business side of things, who had insisted.

'I'm so sorry, Ian,' he said, swallowing his anger, 'I'm dealing with it all as well as I can.'

But he knew the glowing figure could only hear the thumping rhythm of Guns N' Roses through his headphones, and it suited his own purposes just fine. He stepped into the lift, admired his face and elegant appearance in the mirrors on all sides and descended.

THREE

Twenty-five miles away at Derringham Commando Training Barracks, Professor Peter Morris stared morosely from his office window at the line of red-faced, sweating marines completing their ten-mile, forced march. Each had a thick log bearing down on their shoulders, their taut, sinewed forearms strained awkwardly across the top. From the chest up, they looked like Christ-figures hanging from truncated crucifixes. Unbidden, their agonised expressions had dragged Prisoner 105's face back into Morris's inner focus.

It had been almost six months ago that Morris had first entered the place with the most tremendous sense of excitement. It had promised all that was cutting edge about his scientific speciality. Reality had turned out much more leaden and disappointing. He should have guessed it from the heavy-handed, vaguely threatening manner in which he'd been inducted into the top-secret enterprise by the director, no less, for Homeland Security.

'Let's be absolutely clear, Professor Morris, shall we?' Director Phillip Faulkner had intoned. 'You have now signed six copies of the Official Secrets Act. You fully understand the serious penalties for disclosing any of the information given you here today. Is that correct?'

Morris had been recommended as particularly qualified for the work, but Faulkner wasn't so sure. The professor had a nauseating arrogance about him and a six-figure salary. But he was also one of the foremost specialists in his field and had seemed eager to be heading up the project.

'I understand,' Morris replied. 'As I've said, I'll need state-of-the-art facilities and the best personnel available. It's going to be very, very expensive, I'm afraid.'

'Whatever you need, Professor. This project has top priority and an unlimited budget.'

Morris beamed his appreciation. He was back on top again!

'I wouldn't get too euphoric if I were you,' Faulkner had warned him. '"Unlimited budget" means we needed this clarifying by yesterday. I don't care to know the details of how you run this operation. I just need to know if it's authentic.

'Let me also stress to you again that this is specifically a Homeland Security matter. We've chosen Derringham barracks as the base for this project because it happens to be the most secure installation in the West Country. The military authorities here don't need to know anything. As I'm sure you appreciate, the larger the number of people in the loop, the greater the risk of security leaks. You'll answer directly to me and my department alone.'

He placed the signed documents in his valise and rose to leave.

'Probably a load of nonsense,' he said dismissively, 'but, if you get this wrong…' He paused. 'Well, just don't get it wrong. Clear?'

'Crystal,' Morris had stated, smiling.

A fine joke on himself that had been, Morris now reflected, as the curses of the exhausted marines filtered through his open window.

'Crystal clear!'

He'd no more clue now what he was doing, or what this damned thing was, than he'd had when he first stepped through the doors of the facility all those months ago!

FOUR

Ray had arrived back at the office a half-hour later. Leary, clenching his fist closed and dropping a magnifying lens from his eye socket, looked up, furious and guilty.

'Barge in, eh?' he said angrily, scooping up the lens.

'Sorry,' Ray replied awkwardly.

'Look, boy, something's just come up. I'm going to have to get back to Hackney, pronto. Got a little job here while I'm gone.'

Ray had never seen his uncle so energised before. He passed Ray a passport-style photograph of a man, very similar in appearance to the lady who'd just visited, and guides on places to stay in the town.

'This here Zita Truman, looking for her twin brother, see. Get yourself round as many hotels and B&Bs as you can and see if anyone's clocked him. Couple of quid in it for you, son,' he added, winking.

Ray had felt elated. For the first time ever, his uncle was giving him a chance to get involved in some real 'PI' work! The offer of a measly couple of quid wouldn't begin to cover the meter money Ray had already 'lent' him, but who cared?

'When are you back?' Ray asked.

'Make it ten tomorrow and we'll see what you turned up. Here's the key. Lock up when you've finished, boy.'

He bustled off downstairs and Ray heard his car start up and pull away. He sat in Leary's chair and put his feet up on the desk. What he'd just witnessed almost qualified as a miracle: his uncle upright, motivated and moving at speed! He picked up a biro, drew an imaginary drag of smoke from it and, blowing into the air, checked his watch.

'You got twenty-four hours to crack the case, boy,' he said aloud and smiled broadly.

*

By seven that evening his enthusiasm had all but evaporated. Having cycled all over the town and outlying areas, he'd discovered two things. One, that adults gave very little shrift to kids asking them questions; all, with one exception, had been curt and dismissive.

The second discovery was more interesting. It seemed that someone else had been looking for Miss Truman's brother and offering money for the information.

It was actually after 11.30 the following morning when Leary finally showed up. Ray, waiting for him, felt increasingly uneasy. He had a special knack for feeling guilty about letting others down. His mother had left jobs to be done during the Easter holidays and, so far, he'd touched none of them. Returning late from work she'd asked him sarcastically what he'd been doing with himself all day. He seldom told lies but had made things up to avoid mentioning the case. She would have gone berserk!

'Well, what you got?' Leary asked, settling himself in his chair.

'I didn't finish till after seven,' Ray began defensively. 'I've been all over the town. Must have cycled about ten miles.'

'Wow, that's impressive… and if this was a charity bike ride, that'd be tip-top, top notch, wouldn't it, son?' Leary observed. 'But we're on a "little quest" for this Truman feller, ain't we? Now. You seen any sign of him?'

'No… No, I didn't. Sorry.'

'What? Like nothing at all? You make a list of the places you been?'

Ray looked down embarrassed and annoyed with himself. Leary shook his head dolefully.

'Ah, come on, boy! You're really goin' to have to get a bit of drive and oomph about you,' he said, clenching his fists in gee-up style.

Ray suddenly felt his eyes filling. His lack of 'oomph' was something of a constant theme with adults; whatever he attempted seemed to disappoint them. Now, even Uncle Garry was in on the act!

'There was another man asking,' he muttered.

'What other man?'

'I don't know. He'd been around to most of the places. He'd even offered money for information.'

'Did he?' Leary said, rising from his chair. 'Right, boy. Show me where you been, and which ones still need calling on.'

It was at one of the holiday parks that Leary came face to face with his only local rival in the private investigation business, Jonas Warrington. Apart from their occupations and military background, they also shared a mutual loathing of each other.

Warrington, six foot three with cropped hair and full moustache, looked every inch the ex-marine and military policeman he had once been. He had powerful connections in the town too: his brother-in-law, Charlie Manley.

'Well, what do we have here?' Warrington began sarcastically. 'Garry Lazarus, finally risen from the bed.'

'You know what, Oscar, my sides is fair busting! Hilarious. Absolutely, bleedin' hilarious… Listen, you on a missing-person case?' Leary asked.

'Oscar? Who's Oscar?' Warrington asked, puzzled. 'Yeah, I'm on a case, and that's my business, isn't it, Leary? So, I tell you what, do yourself a big fat favour and stay out of my business. There's people in high places backing me, see?'

'People in high places? Right… That'd be the Great Charlie, would it? Up there on his Big Dipper in the Wonderful World of Dismal.'

'Always a cocky answer, haven't you, Leary? I'd watch it if I was you, though. I'm telling you for your own good, see.'

'Ah! That's nice. That's real pally of you, Jonas.'

Warrington made for his car and, as he opened the door, Leary called out, 'Here, Jonas!'

Warrington turned.

'Wipe your nose. There's a bogey on your top lip.'

The man reached for his pocket handkerchief, then stopped himself in time.

'Nah!' continued Leary. 'It's that decomposing rat of a moustache.'

Warrington came back, shaking his finger angrily. 'Listen, Leary, you've got no sense of professional courtesy or ethics. You're just a lazy, cockney, barrow boy who doesn't know his business! There isn't enough work here for two of us, so why don't you just shove off back to where you came from? Let people with a proper sense of professionalism get on and—'

'Ooooh!' Leary moaned suddenly, grabbing his backside, his face contorted with agony.

Warrington faltered. 'What… What's the matter?'

'Oooooh!' groaned Leary again, clutching his buttocks with both hands.

'What is it?' asked Warrington, genuinely concerned.

'Nah! Nothing,' Leary grunted. 'Nothing really, Jonas. Just back off a bit.'

Warrington stepped back a couple of paces.

'Ah! That's better. Only,' Leary suddenly straightened up and smiled, 'you're boring me arse off again.'

'You're just a great, stupid kid, aren't you, Leary!' Warrington shouted as he walked away. 'Waste of time talking to you!'

He got into his car, crunched some gears and drove off.

'Jonas! Jeez! What kind of a lame name's that? Gormless more like. Come on, boy, I'm going to check out some rented stuff I know.'

FIVE

'Jenny, can you ask Mr Manley to step in now, please?'
Gerald Dunstable released the intercom switch and stroked his smooth-shaven chin thoughtfully. He was elegant in a grey, double-breasted suit, silk shirt and tie and handmade shoes. His swept-back, thick, blond hair, with subtle highlights, combined with a carefully toned tan, to give an appearance of health, wealth and athleticism. He was thirty-one years old, loving his life, and it showed!

The Dunstables were landed, affluent and had been major players in the town's affairs for the past 200 years. The last twelve months since Gerald Dunstable's first meeting with the eccentric genius, Ian Vader, however, had opened up possibilities of riches and influence well beyond even his imagination.

Vader had turned up, uninvited, at the Dunstable country house one evening and caused an uproar. The police were about to be called when he'd quietened himself and shown Dunstable technological processes and components on a tablet.

Lunatic or not, there had been an earnestness about him which had intrigued Dunstable. The drawings had been checked out by a friend from his Oxford days, Dr Alastair Stapleton, 'the moron' who was now heading up the research department at Vader International. Stapleton was the acknowledged leader in the field of nanotechnology and had been staggered by the simplicity and depth of the processes shown him; the industrial equivalent, he claimed, of '$E=mc^2$'.

'I've never seen anything remotely like this before. He's using a wholly new branch of organic chemistry for manufacturing! The applications for this technique are frankly astonishing, Gerald; everything from computer chips to pharmaceuticals. I've got to meet this man! He's a genius on an absolutely epic scale!'

Stapleton's subsequent meeting had shown the truth of the adage, 'Never meet your heroes for fear of disappointment'. Except that Stapleton hadn't been disappointed. He'd been patronised, humiliated and finally insulted by the other man.

In Vader's very limited circle of acquaintance, it was only Gerald Dunstable to whom he showed any sign of awareness that human beings, with feelings to hurt, existed outside his own mind-frame. To begin with, Vader had totally surrendered himself over to Dunstable, like a child grateful for the protection and support of a parent. He copied everything Dunstable did and hung on his every word.

There were still difficult times, though, such as the occasion Dunstable had had to present Stapleton with a white toilet seat from his bathroom, upon which Vader had written, in absolutely minuscule writing, the next phase of a construction process. Stapleton had subsequently stated it was sheer, unadulterated brilliance in its elegance and power.

Or the day Dunstable had come home to find the manic Vader with a black permanent marker in each hand, writing meticulously, ambidextrously and furiously, yards and yards of equations across the Versace-decorated dining room walls.

Appearing to have no family, friends or even a permanent roof over his head, Dunstable had invited him to stay at the manor, but the arrangement had quickly become a nightmare, literally a nightmare. For, every night without fail, Vader's high-pitched screams and horrific shrieks as he threw himself, tortured, across his bed, echoed out across the shadowy, darkened grounds of the Dunstable family home.

Dunstable had acquired drugs that seemed to reduce Vader's manic condition and nightly distress but getting the right amount of medication was difficult. Doping him up too much seriously hampered his powers of concentration. Finally, he had hired a mental health nurse, Margaret Welch, who attended his local church. She fussed over Vader and not only sorted out his medication but also indulged his often-bizarre eating and entertainment needs. She was relentlessly cheerful, fawned on Dunstable and secretly loathed Vader, whom she found repulsive and demanding.

Dunstable was also disgusted by the man's neediness and erratic change of moods, for Vader became more challenging and less easy to manage with each passing day.

Finally, he had shifted him out to the penthouse suite at the beach-front office as soon as it was ready.

Vader never left the suite and, when he wasn't working at a frenzied pace, stuffed himself with every variety of food and drink. Following such binges, he would work out ferociously on his gym equipment.

'Ian! Ian!' Dunstable had shouted and waved one day as Vader was sitting on his stationary exercise bike.

He was pedalling like a crimson-faced, sweating maniac; his eyes focused in startling intensity on the mid-distance whilst his headphones banged out the noisiest, most mindless pop music.

'You really should see my physician Dr Cormack. All this eating and then overexercising. It can't be good for you!'

Vader had screeched at him furiously for a full two minutes about his need for privacy, and Dunstable had never broached the subject again. If he wanted to kill himself that was fine with Dunstable, provided he completed the work first.

The rest of his time Vader played with the latest electronic gadgets and games, watching anything up to ten different channels simultaneously on the bank of televisions in his bedroom. He was a genuine, one-off phenomenon and, as far as Gerald Dunstable was concerned, the sooner he could dump this 'fruitcake', the better!

The most impressive and potentially profitable of Vader's breakthroughs was a revolutionary process designed to produce, as Vader bizarrely put it, 'A thousand quantum computer chips as cheaply as a half-pound portion of Cheddar cheese'. News of the development had somehow leaked out, so Dunstable had the largest dot com companies, panicking at the potential destruction of their monopolies, constantly pestering him.

Having to see Manley was another nuisance, but he was proving useful in Vader International's business strategy. It was the first time Dunstable had invited the man over to his office and, because of Manley's unsavoury reputation, he was uncomfortable about it. They usually met at the Lodge or the Conservative Club, but this was something of a crisis.

Manley came in and the two shook hands warmly. They made a considerable contrast: the one tall, easy and sophisticated; the other short, stout, bald and looking every inch the ex-builder made good.

'Morning, Gerry,' Manley greeted cheerily.

The 'Gerry' always irritated Dunstable, but swallowing the vulgarity was a small sacrifice to keep the brute happy. He poured himself and Manley a whisky on the rocks and sat down at his desk. The sea's reflecting sunshine streaming into the room, Manley looked with approval at the elegance and luxury of the office and swivelled his chair to take in the view.

'Very, very nice too, Gerry,' he observed.

'Thank you, Charles,' Dunstable said, smiling. 'Glad you approve.'

'Yeah, well when you've had as little as me, you appreciate the finer things in life, Gerry. Council house in the East End. Ain't exactly The Savoy, is it?'

Dunstable smiled indulgently at his associate but just didn't have the time this morning for the rags-to-riches story, which bored him senseless.

'Yes, you're certainly doing very well for yourself, Charles, but I wonder if we could cut to the chase. Following our telephone conversation, what can you tell me about this man... Leary, is it?'

Manley, taking a notebook from his jacket pocket, began reading from it. 'Yeah. He's a right little toe rag, Gerry. Had a private investigation business in Hackney and moved here a few months back. He's got an office above the butchers on the Strand – one of your properties, Warrington reckons – and family in the town, his ex-sister-in-law, Lorraine Bradnock. She works here at Vader International. Her fifteen-year-old kid hangs out with him.

'Apparently, Leary was a right little tearaway delinquent. Then he suddenly joined up – Devonshire Light Infantry.'

'The Devonshire Light, eh? My father's old regiment,' Dunstable clarified in response to Manley's quizzical expression. 'Actually, that might come in useful – the "Old Comrades Network".'

'Did tours out in Afghanistan and Germany, then spent time in an army detention centre,' Manley continued. 'Got done for some kind of smuggling racket while he was out in Berlin. Involved in some radical, political group at the same time and then got the heave-ho.

'Been drifting from one crappy job to another – security, that sort of thing. Private investigating's his latest little hobby. Bets on the gee-gees, bit of sea fishing now and then and hits the bottle regular down the Legion.

'He's got an old army buddy, a copper in Exeter, and apart from his time in the army, the sister-in-law and nephew, that's his only connections with the area. Jonas reckons he's an idle git, pardon my French; street-smart but a loser no one would ever miss.

'Listen, I know the type, Gerry – wide boy. Bung him a couple of hundred quid and get him out your hair. It's all in here,' he said, passing the book across.

He paused. 'It's this Truman you want sorting, Gerry. I mean, who is she?'

'I'm not sure,' Dunstable said, frowning. 'I only know she could upset some very important plans. Tell me, is Warrington available for further work?'

'Oh, yeah,' replied Manley. 'He does exactly what I tell him.'

'Good.' Dunstable passed Manley another top-up of his drink.

'Listen, Charles, I want this handling very, very discreetly, so no strong-arm tactics, please. And,' he looked Manley full in the eyes with a coldness which briefly surprised the rougher man, 'no questions.'

'Manley Leisure and Property Services are doing very, very nicely thanks to you, Gerry, old son. I'll do things exactly the way you want 'em.'

'Thank you,' said Dunstable. 'I won't forget this. I'd also be grateful if you could join me in a little visit to our Mr Leary this afternoon.'

'Suits me, Gerry.'

'And now, Charles,' Dunstable continued, 'about this prime piece of land you've just acquired. I think Vader International would be very happy to purchase it from you.'

Manley laughed loudly. 'Well, that *is* good news. Very fortunate timing, eh, Gerry? Here's to a long association and success.'

He got up, reached across the desk and clinked his glass with Dunstable's.

'Timing is all,' Dunstable said, smiling broadly at him.

What a perfectly ghastly type Manley is, he thought, and moved him up his mental schedule for future dumping. When the time was right, of course.

SIX

As they drove away from their latest visit to yet another flat, Ray, who'd been pondering the matter of Warrington's threat, asked if he could do what he'd said.

'Kick me off the case? Well, Warrington's a twerp, but he ain't what I call malignant. His brother-in-law, Porky Manley, though, real piece of scum. Jack had a run-in with him. He's got muscle backing him.'

'Are you going to stop after this?' Ray asked.

'Nah, son! I'm making serious, serious cash on this one… And then there's other considerations too.'

He looked serious and solemn. 'You know, boy, all my life people been calling me an idle good-for-nothing. Well, implying it really, 'cos most ain't got the guts to say it to your face. Way I see it, I got a real chance now to show 'em what kind of mettle Garry Leary's really made of. Prove meself to 'em all… What do you make of that, son?'

'Well, that's… that's great!' said Ray, smiling as he encountered a wholly new side to his uncle's character.

'Jeez, son,' Leary commented, shaking his head, 'you got one hell of a lot to learn, haven't you? Listen, I've just sold you a shovel-an-a-half load of high-class fertiliser there. You ever hear someone getting all pompous and up themselves, you watch out, see? 'Cos they're definitely playing you for a mug.

'See, there's two basic rules in life, boy, that no sod ever tells you. That's 'cos most of 'em don't get it 'emselves, see. Rule number one: don't take nothing anyone says to you at face value. And I mean nothing. And rule number two: it's every beggar for himself in this life, no matter what highfalutin cobblers people spout at you.'

He looked across at Ray. 'See, most of life is smoke, mirrors and what I call "prestidigitation". There's a word, eh? Prestidigitation. What magicians do, son. Sleight of hand. Misdirection. Works like this, see. While you're cooing over the bunny rabbit I pulled out the top hat in this hand, I'm pilfering your back pocket with the other one. Yeah? You'd be surprised, boy, how much of life is smoke, mirrors and abra-bleedin'-cadabra.

'Years back, I done a tour out in Afghanistan. That's when I started to lose me smoke-coloured specs. Had blokes coming up to me when I got back, shaking me hand, and calling me a hero. Me, a hero!

'Had its good side, like; free drinks all round. 'Course they hadn't got a clue what I was doing out there. Didn't want to know neither. We was shooting and blowing up peasants just like them, see. You know, ordinary beggars. 'Course, out there, we called 'em "Ragheads", but that was just about getting a bit of distance, so we didn't feel too bad about the stuff we was doing.

'Brutal, brutal stuff, son. You know, we never got nowhere near the top dogs who was actually running the show and making a fortune off narcotics.

'Anyway, when I quit the army for civvy street and need a bit of help, suddenly, no beggar's interested. It was all, "Man-up-get-off-your-idle-backside-and-stop-sponging-off-the-state" tosh.

'See, while I was your average mutt following orders and doing me bit for God, Queen and country, everything was hunky-dunky-dory. Minute I start asking what I'm doing out there, all them wallahs at the top come down on me hard, like muggers at a blindman's convention. 'Cept they're too smart and posh to kick your head in. Too obvious, like. They just use all the laws what they, or their old dads, made up and put the squeeze on you. Then, you either break, or fall in line.

'Yeah! Good, old British Blighty's built on prestidigitation – church, corporations, finance, politicians, lawyers. You name 'em. That's how they all get along, saying one thing to your face then doing something different round the back.

'Your real pros are the middle and upper classes, see. Very smooth, smarmy and whip-crack sharp. That's where all the brains behind the prestidigitation comes from, boy. You think a High Court judge's Percy ain't as titchy as yours in a cold shower? Just stick him in a red robe and wig and he's cock-of-the-walk.

'Prestidigitation; changes any beggar or thing into whatever them at the top decide they want 'em to be!'

He paused. 'You know, son, you really are going to have to wise up a bit sharpish now you got your mum to think of.'

Ray sat in a mildly depressed silence. Uncle Garry's take on life wasn't exactly uplifting, was it? Also, that idea had just popped into his head again. He could see how often his uncle mentioned his mother, and it was always fondly. Ray wondered if Uncle Garry was planning to be his next dad.

And that didn't seem like such a great idea, really.

They pulled up in front of a rundown Victorian house where an old man was sitting outside on a weather-worn bench. Leary went across to him.

'Alright, pops. I'm a private investigator. You know a bloke at Flat 2 looking like this?'

He brought out his credentials and the photo. The man studied the picture and then looked suspicious and uncomfortable.

'He's gone,' was all he said, an Irish accent apparent.

'Yeah?' Leary, delighted, took in the old man's frayed cuffs and grubby, buttoned-up shirt collar, and pulled out a £20 note from his wallet. 'Anything you can tell me about him, Mr er… and I'll be very grateful,' he said, smiling.

The man looked furtively around. 'It's Flanagan… I got told to wind me neck in.'

'What?' Leary asked, puzzled.

'Mind me own business.'

'Right… Well, how about another couple on top of that one?' Leary asked, flourishing two more notes.

Flanagan looked momentarily doubtful, then stole a glance at the £60 and moved in closer to Leary who had sat down next to him.

'I never told you none of this,' he began nervously. 'Feller's name was Truman, I'm thinking. 'Bout six months ago it'll be, vanloads of coppers and soldiers turned up here in the dead of night. All decked up in some kind of white, hooded overalls with gas masks over their faces. Didn't hear them get in the house. Just heard some noise in the hallway, then they battered down his door.

'My flat's opposite, see, so I came out. They were just plain nasty. Told me to feck off and keep me door and mouth shut. Well, I know from bitter experience that you don't argue with them lads. Bit later I took a quick look out the front window and saw four of 'em carrying him out, face-up with tape across his mouth, one on each of his arms and legs. He wasn't struggling or nothing. They put him in one of the vans and drove off with a police escort. Real quiet like. No sirens.'

'Any idea where they took him?' Leary asked, putting the money into his hand.

'No. Bit later the rest of them left. Stripped the place. I looked in the *Gazette* that Thursday to see if there was anything about him there. Nothing. Then, about a week later two coppers called around. Was all about some big international drugs deal, they told me.'

'Here, any chance you could let me in for a little shufti round this flat? I'd make it worth your while,' Leary suggested.

'No. No, it's been boarded up since – metal gate, alarm system, the lot – and I don't want no trouble. Had more than enough in my lifetime. Odd though, isn't it? Mind, he was right peculiar. Not the full shilling. Coming and going all times of the day and night... Funny sounds sometimes coming out of the room. I tell you, I'm no eejit; yer man was no drug dealer, that's for sure. Looked more like a Holy Joe.'

'Yeah. Well, thanks, pops. Keep this to yourself. Right?'

Flanagan nodded. 'Fine by me. Like I said, I don't want no trouble. Always remember to forget, that's my motto.'

'Oh,' asked Leary as he stood up, 'did this Truman bloke ever have a natter with you about anything?'

'Strange though it is, now you mention it, I never heard him speak a word. Never made any fuss when they took him away neither. His nose was bleeding, and he had all these cuts and red marks over his face, but he looked as calm as a babby brimming with mother's milk. Sure, it takes all sorts to make a world. It really does. Much obliged for the craic, mister.'

Leary got back in the car and rolled himself a cigarette. 'I tell you what, he was scared enough, wasn't he? Still, that's it for me then. Case investigated, mission accomplished, cash in the bag! Yes!'

He winked across at Ray who thought his uncle seemed to have picked a really easy way to make a living.

And then five minutes later, they'd entered Leary's office and found Dunstable, Manley and Warrington waiting for them.

SEVEN

It was just after three o'clock when Ray got back home from his uncle's office following that embarrassing scene with Mr Dunstable and his associates. He'd been lying on the bed feeling guilty about deceiving his mother, so had decided to do some of the jobs she'd left. He'd even fetched the newspapers, brushes and tin of emulsion paint he'd picked with her to decorate his bedroom with. He recalled how enthusiastic he had had to pretend to be when they were choosing it, just to keep her happy.

He started painting, frustrated at how the stuff trickled down his fingers and barely covered over the wallpaper pattern beneath it. Wishing he hadn't bothered, he went back to lying on the bed.

The front door suddenly opened, and Ray sat bolt upright. He'd meant to set the table and get a microwave meal ready for their tea. His mother was a couple of hours earlier than usual. He clattered down the stairs and suddenly stopped.

She was standing at the bottom, looking furiously up at him. Then she let him have both barrels!

She'd been summoned by her manager at Vader International who had complimented her on her hard work, but then asked, very sympathetically, if there were any family problems troubling her. Apparently, her son, Raymond, had been calling around to places in the town and making something of a nuisance of himself. Of course, she believed that Mrs Bradnock would never encourage her son to undertake such potentially 'hazardous' activities. So, would she like to leave work early and talk with him, or would fewer hours in the job give her the time she needed to sort things out?

Mrs Bradnock told Ray she'd felt humiliated, lied to and a bad mother. She absolutely banned him from going anywhere near his uncle's office. She asked Ray how he would like to manage on the money she earned, and had it ever occurred to him what Dad leaving her for a younger woman felt like. Then she'd started to cry.

It was one of the nightmare scenarios Ray had always dreaded; his mother looking vulnerable in a way he'd never seen before. He'd gone to comfort her, but she'd pushed him away, told him to get to his room and had followed him up the stairs.

And, oddly enough, that had kind of saved him from plunging totally into despair. Because he felt, at some level, that she didn't really care all that much for him, if truth were told. That if she'd really felt something, she would have opened up and welcomed whatever communication, affection or comfort he could offer. But, she hadn't. There was an odd sense of coldness about the way she treated him, and always had been when he considered it.

He had lain on his bed, listening to her gradually subsiding sobs through the bedroom wall. He felt utterly confused because none of what had happened had impacted on him the way he felt it should. He should be feeling terribly, terribly guilty about upsetting her. This was his mother after all. What kind of monster was he if he didn't really feel that way?

Wasn't that just another confirmation that he was a straight-up 'psycho' and emotionally dead shell?

He'd finally heard her emerge, move around downstairs in the kitchen and come back up. Pausing outside his door, Ray had looked hopefully at it, but there was just a plate of sandwiches and a glass of milk on the landing when he finally dared to investigate.

As the darkness and depression of night came, the historical narrative of Ray's life so far confirmed yet again that he really was the worst human being in history; an idle, deceiving, third-rate drifter, much like his uncle. He wasn't sporty, brainy or remotely attractive. He was a talentless, work-shy, socially inept, isolated 'no-mark'!

But then, some other notion of himself would appear in his mind, suggesting that perhaps, at some level, he really wasn't so bad, for he didn't actually feel awful about himself all the time. Didn't that reinforce his status as some kind of utterly confused, schizophrenic, 'mental' bighead? Or did it suggest he was, somehow, better than he'd been led to expect of himself?

If Ray had had any notion about how many other people felt similarly confused most of the time, he might not have felt so desolate or uniquely appalling… because he would have had 'company'. But, unfortunately, everyone around him, apart from the ROSLA block girls, seemed to be functioning just fine; and that made him outstandingly, dreadfully weird!

There was a counsellor at school he would have liked to speak to about how bewildered and rotten he felt, but he didn't seem to be disruptive, loud or disturbed enough to qualify for an appointment. And the concept of asking for one on his own initiative was simply beyond his comprehension. As far as he could tell, people were just expected to get on with things, and anything less suggested a real lack of character and backbone.

He was caught, though he didn't know it, in another brilliant, humanly manufactured paradox: you felt like a useless waste of space and would confirm the truth of that feeling by asking for help to try and sort it!

He remained staring at the ceiling, and it was the early hours of the morning when he finally fell asleep.

Waking with a start, he checked his watch – 8.46am. He raced downstairs but his mother had already gone. On the kitchen table was a note:

> 'I think we need some time and space away from each other. I've asked your dad to have you over to his for next week. I think it's for the best.'

Ray sat down slowly at the formica-topped kitchen table, his shoulders started to shake and, even before he realised what he was doing, he sobbed big sobs, his forehead resting on the cold, red surface, like he hadn't done since he was a toddler.

EIGHT

Garry Leary, eyes red and bleary, had opened his office late. He'd drunk more than had been wise, even for him, the night before because the meeting with Dunstable and Manley had seriously unsettled him.

He'd had many insulting things said to him in his time, but the boy's presence and Dunstable's crack about him being 'a chip off the old block' had caught him completely off-guard. Throwing the money back now struck him, in the cold light of day, as being a great deal more about bravado than good sense.

If the kid hadn't been there, Leary would have comfortably settled for Dunstable's pay-off, the substantial deposit the Truman woman had given him, and an easy life. Pride had prompted him into that show of defiance, and pride, like principles, was an expensive commodity in life. Most people knuckled under because it was stupid and dangerous to do otherwise. If you stuck your head above the parapet someone, somewhere, was bound to take a shot at it.

The boy was late this morning, Leary noted; often he was waiting for him out in the corridor. Funny kind of kid; nothing like Phil or himself. Sort of 'wet' really, but okay for all that. Lorraine and his brother seemed to have brought up a real decent lad, and if there was a vacancy in Lorraine's life and she was remotely interested. Well…

The Truman woman was due in ten minutes. Now that was a seriously mental case! Wealthy, but weird as hell!

He heard steps on the stairs and landing, then a gentle tap on the door. She was a few minutes early.

'Yeah. Come in,' Leary called out.

A refined and kindly-looking man in a dark suit and overcoat entered, smiling.

'Mr Leary? Good morning to you. I'm James Henderson from Henderson and Sons, solicitors,' he introduced himself. 'I wonder if I might have a word with you?'

'Sure, Mr Henderson. Have a seat. What can I do for you?'

'Look, this is all rather awkward, but I'm afraid there appears to have been an oversight in your tenancy arrangements,' Henderson began delicately.

'Oh yeah?' Leary replied.

'Yes. The… um, the tenancy agreement for your office unfortunately doesn't appear to cover your business. It's private investigation work, isn't it?' he asked, narrowing his eyes.

'That so? I been here a few months now, Mr Henderson. What's the problem?'

Henderson took documents from his briefcase and placed them carefully on the desk so that Leary could read them.

'Well, let me explain it this way, Mr Leary. If you look just here, you'll see the letting contract stipulates that the agent has the right to cancel the agreement, if your business contravenes certain protocols. Now, I'm afraid I have to notify you that it is his intention to so do.'

'Come again?'

'My apologies, Mr Leary. Look, I can explain it more clearly by referencing the documents here,' Henderson suggested kindly, leaning across the desk to point out the relevant sections. 'If you look there, for example, Clause Four, Subsection A states that there are certain… limitations regarding the nature of the work that can be discharged within these premises. I'm rather afraid it could be interpreted as negligence on your part for not informing the agent fully of the property's intended usage. It's known as "*Condicio sine qua non*" in the original Latin.'

He looked up and laughed at the apparent foolishness of the law on occasions.

'It's a general principle that goes back as far as Richard the Lionheart, interestingly, and I'm so sorry to get a little technical, Mr Leary, but can you see? There, there and there.'

Henderson indicated the appropriate paragraphs.

'Yeah.' Leary paused and then looked the man full in the face. 'You ever tried English, Mr Henderson?'

'Pardon?'

'Ever tried talking it? English?'

'Mr Leary, please, I do appreciate this may have come as something of a shock.' Henderson smiled sympathetically

'Yeah. Not really, Mr Henderson. So, what's the upshot?'

'Pardon?'

'When do you want me out?' Leary asked, cutting to the chase.

'Er… Well… End of the week, I'm afraid. Sorry, that does seem a little sudden.'

'It does, don't it? You got anywhere else local?' Leary asked, already guessing the answer.

'Erm, no, unfortunately. We took the liberty of phoning other agents on your behalf to ask if they had any possibilities in the area. I'm afraid we drew a blank.'

'Well, there's a surprise. That was good of you, Mr Henderson, putting out the word for us amongst your pals,' Leary observed, pleasantly. 'Tell me, though, did the Great Man give you any hints where I can beggar off to? You know, Outer Hebrides. Blindfolded at midnight in me slippers and jim-jams on the M5 fast lane. Maybe six foot horizontal under his country house patio?'

'Oh, it's nothing to do with Mr Dunstable,' Henderson replied, laughing, his gaze back on the documents.

'For a solicitor, Mr Henderson, you're a bit on the crap side at lying. I never mentioned Dunstable. Everybody been having a little chinwag about me down the Rotary Club. Or was it the Conservative Club?'

'Mr Leary, I really don't like what's being implied here, and you really should appreciate the seriousness of such a charge. Technically, that's slander and could be challenged in a court of law.'

'Hold your horses! I ain't implying nothing… So, when do I get me 800 quid back?'

'Eight hundred…?' Henderson queried.

'Yeah. Me deposit on the premises.'

Henderson looked troubled, his forehead frowning. He really hadn't wanted to push Leary this hard, but the other men had insisted.

'Well… unfortunately, because you failed to notify us fully of the property's intended usage, the deposit becomes subject to new interpretation. The letting agent can claim it as compensation for rent lost, as a result of your vacating the premises earlier than agreed.'

'Yeah, but I'm only vacating them 'cos he's kicking me out, right?' Leary countered.

'Well, er, that depends on how you interpret the overall facts of the case. A court of law would view it very differently, I'm afraid.'

'Um,' Leary began, 'interesting. Can I have another look at those clauses and subsections again, Mr Henderson?'

'Of course, Mr Leary,' Henderson replied, smiling and fully confident that a man of Leary's clearly limited education would find no means of challenging him.

Leary took the documents and began reading through them.

'Yeah. Yeah. Uh-huh,' he said at intervals as he made his way through the papers.

'Very interesting,' he said finally, leaning back in his chair. 'I'm getting a bit technical meself here, Mr Henderson, but I just noticed that, if you take the first or second or third letter of each alternate word in those clauses and subsections here, you get…'

Leary picked up a biro and began writing a line of capital letters at the bottom of the paper.

'See? There's an L. Yep. Then we got a consonant. A vowel. Then there's an N… Here, this is just like that

Countdown. We got an apostrophe, then a vowel, two more consonants and an E stuck on the end. Do you see?'

'Sorry?' Henderson frowned at the papers, puzzled.

'Yeah, that explains it, Mr Henderson. There in black and white,' Leary said, circling the letters and punctuation mark into two separate words. 'Not Lionheart. "Lyin' Arse".'

Henderson's expression had been changing from benevolent to suspicious and finally hostile as he caught on to Leary's game.

'And what, exactly, is your point, Mr Leary?' he asked coldly.

'Well, let's just "sum it up" as you'd say in court, Mr Henderson. You've just pitched me a bit of legal jargon. You've followed through with some sand chucked in me eyes about Latin and Dickie Lionheart and protocols, and now you're serving me up a bit of, what I call, prestidigitation. All done with enormous charm and a big fat smile, of course. And the verdict, I have to tell you, Mr Henderson, is "*Bootus backsidicus*".'

'What?' Henderson questioned, leaning forward, his brow furrowed.

'*Bootus backsidicus*. That's the original Leary for "move your lyin' arse before I kick it down them stairs".'

He stood up and walked across to the door, holding it open.

Henderson was outraged. 'Do you know, Mr Leary, I have never been spoken to like that in all my years in the legal profession!'

'Well, I tell you what, Henderson, if you could pop round here tomorrow morning round about ten, I'll try and make it two in a row for you.'

'That's a threat!' Henderson accused, reddening.

'Nah, it ain't a threat, Mr Henderson. It's a sure-fire promise. So, I'd move it if I was you.'

Henderson collected together his papers and strode to the door. 'I was told to expect an awkward customer, Mr Leary. They didn't tell me you were an outright fool,' he said before leaving.

'Yeah, one of them qualifications I like to keep to meself, pal!' Leary called after him.

So, it's starting already, is it? Leary thought, sitting at his desk. *Now where is that bloody Truman woman?*

NINE

Although it was only the Wednesday of the first week of his Easter holidays, Ray felt he was hating it even more than school-time! He was bored, isolated and living in a very uncomfortable household. Coming home from his paper round he determined to try and raise the emotional temperature to something more than freezing, by making amends to his mother. He'd done all the jobs and had the meals ready as soon as she came through the door. She looked exhausted but became less cold and distant with him as the evening progressed.

His father rang, the first time in months Ray hadn't had to initiate the contact. He knew what was coming; the man sounded distant and irritable. After a few opening questions about Ray's progress at school, he had then launched into him about his behaviour and attitudes. Ray needed to get a grip; to be less selfish and self-centred. He would be leaving school soon and still didn't seem to have a clue what he wanted to do with his life. He needed to grow up! Sharpish! Mr Bradnock had also strongly hinted that Uncle Garry wasn't his first choice of mentor for his son, though he gave no specific reason why.

The man finished by saying that he would pick him up from Birmingham New Street station the following Monday and had not sounded terribly enthusiastic at the prospect. Then he asked to be passed back to Mum.

Ray felt as if he had let everybody down by not shouldering the now empty role of 'man of the house'. Even though nobody had ever actually asked him to. Certainly not Dad, who'd vacated it!

As he left the room, he could hear his mother's tone of voice as she talked to his father, and what struck him was how easy she sounded with him. The pair had always sounded easy and together when Ray was deemed to be at fault.

He gave his mother as cheery a goodnight as he could muster, went up to his bedroom and lay, fully clothed, under the duvet. He drifted off to sleep sometime around one in the morning, convinced, yet again, that he probably, actually, was the biggest waste of space ever to have walked on two legs.

At just after three in the morning his mother received a phone call from his uncle. Mugged on his way home from the British Legion, Leary had been in Accident and Emergency when the police had called there. Receiving a tip-off, they had gained an emergency warrant to search his office and had discovered two bags of cannabis and various tablets and pills in the bottom filing-cabinet drawer. He was due at the magistrates' court that morning and was asking if she would stand bail for him.

Mrs Bradnock had come into Ray's room, woken him, and asked him to swear on the family bible to tell her the truth. She demanded he tell her everything that had happened over the previous days. Ray told her what little he knew but refrained from mentioning the incident in the office. Some instinct told him to keep it from her. He was trying to be 'the man' everyone was telling him to be, which meant protecting his mother from information that might distress her.

That was weird, he reflected. Perhaps withholding the truth, or 'lying' as children understood it, was pretty important in the grown-up world.

In the morning his mother phoned in sick and had then gone to attend his uncle's court appearance. She'd looked ill and tired, and for the first time, Ray had noticed the wisps of grey in her hair. He'd wanted to comfort her, but she was still distant with him. He wasn't sure if he was upset for himself or her, so had kept his feelings under wraps. Perhaps that was another important bit about growing up – never letting anyone see how you really felt.

When his mother returned, she said his uncle had looked in a bad way. As a result of the drugs raid he'd been given immediate notice to quit his flat and office, and someone had vandalised his car. He was bailed till next month to answer the charges. She said she felt sorry for him, but he seemed to have 'brought it all on himself'. She absolutely insisted that Ray keep away from him.

There were several lousy things Ray was now facing. The fact was that his uncle's tatty office had been the only place that offered escape from a miserable, lonely, humdrum existence. Now he was banned from even that small consolation!

Secondly, he felt a confusing mixture of shame and guilt about the man. Uncle Garry's awkwardness in the office had shown a vulnerability Ray had never suspected. He worried that the man's defiant performance had been put on for his benefit!

Finally, Ray was just plain shaken by what he'd seen in the space of a mere two days. If these men could mangle the life of a tough-nut like his uncle, what couldn't they do to a fifteen-year-old's and his mother's?

His head might have continued to spin with all this confusion and hurt for weeks, months or, indeed, the rest of his time on Earth. But then, the next day he'd seen Miss Zita Truman again and, unknown to him, his life, which already wasn't that great, would really begin to unravel.

TEN

It was early on the Thursday morning with a bright, fresh sun shining on the sea and promenade. Ray, having delivered his newspapers, was delaying his return home. He still felt bad about abandoning his uncle, but recognised he had little option. He had headed down to the seafront briefly, before returning home to prepare his mother some breakfast – his latest peace offering to her.

The sky was magnificent – turquoise-clear with layers of rose-coloured clouds. Ray sat for a moment mindlessly looking out to sea when he suddenly felt the concrete bench's thick wooden slats creak and flex downwards. Unaware of anyone nearby, he turned his head and found himself looking directly into the stranger's eyes. They were an intense green colour.

'I am Zita Truman. I saw you with Mr Leary. You are...?' the woman asked.

Her voice was calm, quiet, and vaguely foreign sounding.

'Er... Ray... Raymond.'

'Well, Raymond, it is inadvisable for one to see Mr Leary in his office, but it is vital that one meets him,' she continued. 'I would be very grateful if you could pass on this contact number and the further payment that was promised.'

'Yeah… Sure,' Ray replied.

Although a little eccentric in her appearance and manner, there was a kindliness and respect in her attitude towards him that was so unlike most of the grown-ups he encountered in his daily life.

She passed the items to Ray, rose and, as she did so, the bench seemed to creak and flex up again, as if some great weight had been removed.

She smiled pleasantly at him before leaving. 'Thank you, Raymond. This is most gracious.'

In a few moments she had disappeared around the bend of the promenade leading to the Cove, her fluid movement remarkably graceful.

Ray examined the two pieces of paper in his hand. One had a mobile telephone number written, with meticulous neatness, on it; the other was scrunched up. Looking guiltily about him, he opened it. Something shiny flew out and landed under the bench. Lying down on the concrete to retrieve it, he saw something catch the light and stretched his arm under. It felt sharp and he finally managed to pick it up between his fingernails. Withdrawing his arm slowly, he sat upright and dropped the object into the palm of his hand.

There, sparkling with multi-faceted brilliance, lay a beautiful diamond stone.

ELEVEN

At seven-thirty that evening Garry Leary was sitting slumped in a deck chair in a beach hut. He enjoyed sea fishing and this place had been his personal, private retreat. A picnic table had a camping Gaz light resting on it, the remains of a takeaway, a rusty pub ashtray full of stubs, his tobacco pouch, cigarette papers, and a bottle of whisky and plastic cup. His fishing gear, belongings and other beach paraphernalia had been dumped in the corner behind him. The light from the lamp was a sickly yellow and the air, starved of oxygen, was stale and smoky with traces of whisky in it.

He groaned each time he moved – the result of two cracked ribs. The whisky had made him maudlin but not yet drunk. He reached forward for the bottle again and gritted his teeth to prepare for the pain. Those beggars had done one hell of a job on him!

He'd been crossing the open, green space in the centre of the town after an evening at the club, when they'd jumped him from behind. Some enormous gorilla had lifted him clean off the ground. The worst part had been the suffocating black canvas bag put over his head first, while his arms were held, and they worked him over. Nothing to mark his face, but carefully targeted to cause maximum pain.

He could still smell the musty canvas.

The last punch had caught him right in the solar plexus, knocking all the wind out of him.

'He's had enough,' a deep, gruff voice above his head had stated, and he'd been dropped to the ground. But someone else had arrived, disagreed, and given him three solid kicks in the side. That was when he'd heard the ribs crack.

'Toe rag!' spoken with spite and contempt heavy in it. The bag had been pulled off his head and they'd all walked off in eerie silence. He had lain face down in the dew-damp grass, doggy smells and darkness, agonising to get his breath back. Finally, he'd staggered to his feet and got a taxi to hospital.

That had been only the start of his troubles!

Sitting in the gloom he contemplated what had been done to his life. In just three short days all his grand and golden plans had been turned to dirt. Kicked out of his office and flat, he now faced serious charges of drug possession and dealing. His car's bonnet and roof had been covered with paint stripper; the doors dented. That had a professional look about it too, the car damaged but still serviceable enough to be driven one way: out of town.

Then, of course, there was Lorraine and the boy. Leary had seen a chance, a faint one, but still a chance to take his life in a whole new direction. He'd always had a soft spot for his sister-in-law, little time for his brother and a wish to have a family of his own. Married years ago, when in the army, he'd come home one day to find his wife upstairs with his best mate.

Typical!

Yeah, his old man had been dead right to tell him he would never amount to much. The drunken old basket had always had more time for Phil, his brother. He'd given hidings to both sons but never seemed to regret the ones he gave Garry. Still, as Leary himself always said, 'That's life, so get on with it!'

Trouble was that was easier said than done. He'd known he was asking for it when he stood up to Dunstable and Manley but had never anticipated that the bill for his defiance would arrive so promptly, or at such devastating personal cost. Working in Hackney hadn't been a doddle, but the speed he was being driven out of this place! 'Course, it only took a couple of powerful swine in a town this small to turn your whole life upside down.

He cursed the day that Truman woman had walked through his office door. The case she'd brought had seemed simple enough and the lady herself even simpler, if not a little 'touched' in the head. The diamond given him as an upfront payment had been valued by his jeweller pal in Hackney. Two carats and as perfect a specimen as Harry Sharples had ever seen in his life. He estimated its value at between £10,000 to £15,000!

Truman had insisted he take it. Money no object, she'd said. She had promised three more of them: one as investigations progressed and two more when her brother was located. That meant a payment of somewhere between £40,000 and £60,000!

For a missing-person case! He'd hardly ever earned that much in a year, and this was all cash in hand! He could have flogged them to Harry, cleared his debts and still had plenty to make himself a genuinely attractive prospect for Lorraine. And now?

Well, for starters, Zita Bloody Truman hadn't come to see him when she'd said. In fact, she'd disappeared off the radar altogether! Dropped into his life with the prospect of riches then dropped him in the middle of... What?

What was so important about this Truman feller?

His mobile phone rang. He hadn't had a call from anyone in days. It was Lorraine's landline number. He tensed up, cleared his throat and shook his head to clear it.

'Uncle Garry?'

It was the boy. He shouldn't be speaking to him; Lorraine had made that very clear.

'What is it, boy? I'm busy,' he said brusquely.

'I saw the woman this morning... that Miss Truman. She wants to meet up with you, but not at your office. She's... she's left you some things.'

Leary was furious. *So, the old cow has finally shown up, has she? Well, she's going to get it! And how!* he thought.

'I don't know where you are,' Ray added.

Leary tried to weigh up his next move. Getting the boy to come to the hut would be going against Lorraine's express commands. On the other hand, that side of his life was finished anyway. She would never let him into her little family again. And then...

And then it suddenly struck him that he really wanted to see the kid!

Oh, he was a bit wet now and then. Sure! But he was also straight, pleasant, genuine company. You didn't have to waste time working out what he really meant. Leary didn't know many other people of his acquaintance he could say that about. So, he'd see him this last time and tell him of his plans to return to Hackney.

'I'm in a beach hut down the Cove. Number 9. Got a yellow door. When's it safe to come down, son?' he asked.

'Mum's working late again tonight. I… I can come down now.'

'Right, I'll see you then, boy.'

The boy had sounded nervy. In fact, when Leary came to think about it, he always did sound that way. He momentarily wondered why, but then dismissed it.

'Toughen up!' was the answer.

*

Ray had spent all day thinking of nothing else but how he was going to square his conscience with disobeying his mother's clear instructions not to see Uncle Garry, and yet seeing him all the same. He'd only just got himself almost back into her good books and now he was risking all that for someone, he suspected, who didn't really care that much about him anyway.

The man had just called him 'boy' for the umpteenth time. It was always either 'boy' or 'son'. As if he couldn't be bothered to remember his name or, even worse, didn't know what it was!

Ray had finally justified to himself seeing Uncle Garry because it would be his last time. On top of that he was carrying a diamond in his pocket a strange woman had given him, and it was obviously worth a lot of money. He just wanted to hand it over to Uncle Garry and get out of all this.

'Pronto!' as his uncle would say.

TWELVE

Professor Morris had probably just had the worst day of his career, if not his life. Director for Homeland Security, Phillip Faulkner, had turned up unannounced at the facility earlier that morning. Arrived just like that, accompanied only by a single Special Branch bodyguard/driver. High-ranking government officials never, ever did 'spontaneous' visits. Anything that had a whiff of spontaneity about it had usually been well planned in advance. It was intended to convey a sense of crisis, urgency and dissatisfaction to whomever they felt needed a motivating kick up the backside. Or a final boot into the long grass!

Morris was in the midst of another long, weary and heated briefing with the team when Faulkner suddenly appeared in the doorway. He hadn't been anywhere near the place since Morris had signed the official papers all those months back. The team had been discussing the results from the latest genome analysis, which were as inconsistent and confusing as every other aspect of the damned project.

Mackenzie and Brint, in particular, were being as disrespectful as they had ever dared be. In scientific discussions there was a blurred line between legitimate, critical debate and downright contemptuous undermining, and those two regularly, definitely crossed it. Mackenzie was the 'lead pilot' and Brint the sly, underhand 'wingman' in the attacks. Most disturbingly for Morris was the fact that other team members were starting to ingest the spirit of rebellion and contempt at large.

'Look,' Mackenzie was saying to the accompaniment of nodding heads as Faulkner arrived, 'if you insist on giving us only ten or twenty per cent of the data available, how are we supposed to make sense of the readings? We're either respected scientists here or bog-standard, overqualified lab technicians. I'm not being both, and I have to tell you, Morris, that others around this table feel precisely the same way. Currently, we're not even starting to—'

Mackenzie stopped mid-sentence and looked quizzically at Morris; he'd never seen Faulkner before.

'Don't let me interrupt your discussions,' Faulkner had said.

'Er... yes?' Morris began, unclear as to how he should address his superior in the presence of his colleagues, who had no idea of Faulkner's title and role in the project. 'Er... What can I do for you?'

'Your office, Morris,' Faulkner had stated brusquely, pointing down the corridor.

If Faulkner had deliberately set out to further undermine Morris in front of his subordinates, he couldn't have devised a better strategy. Talking to him as if he were some damned skivvy requiring a dressing-down! The subsequent discussions between the two men had been extremely unpleasant.

'You're putting me in an impossible position!' Morris declared, his face red with frustration at Faulkner's unwillingness, or inability, to comprehend what he was up against. 'You saw what they were like!'

'Morris, you're being paid at least double what I earn at the Ministry, so don't whine to me about lacking basic management skills. This is your team. These are all your people. You chose them, and at considerable cost to the taxpayer.'

'But, if you won't let me tell them what you suspect we're dealing with, how can I possibly expect to get their full understanding and co-operation?' the professor demanded.

'Morris, five months ago, in this very office you asked for state-of-the-art facilities and an unlimited budget. I gave you both, together with your own choice of personnel. In return you promised me results. Some definite, concrete conclusion as to whether this subject was genuine or not. Our informant on the inside can't believe how slowly you're working, or how pathetic progress has been. They're also very, very concerned that events may be moving beyond our control.'

'Meaning?' Morris questioned.

'If I knew that, Morris, I wouldn't have set off from London at seven in the morning and driven 200-odd miles to get here! You've got precisely two more weeks to get me a definitive answer, then I'm going to have to assign someone else to lead this. You've heard of Fitzpatrick?'

'Well, of course I have! You seriously want to hand this on to Fitzpatrick? The woman's an ambitious charlatan!'

'Yes, I'm sure she is, but she gets results, Morris, she gets results. Look, it's simple: either the prisoner down the corridor is what our informant, "Cheryl", says he is, or you're making me look like the biggest bloody idiot in the annals of National Security... Two weeks, Morris. Then, you're for the high jump.'

High jump! Bloody idiot! Morris reflected later as he prepared to make the phone call to Ginnie, his wife, who had been expecting him home at seven-thirty, an hour ago.

Yet another overnight stay at the barracks! Who was it that was due for cocktails and savouries? Camilla, the gallery owner, and Penny, the sculptress, together with their partners?

'Why don't you take a bloody mortgage out on the place?' Ginnie demanded. 'You spend more time there than you do here!'

Morris felt even more conflicted because he would have to 'cross the line' again with the subject this evening. It was a very delicate line between torture and striving for truth; particularly because the whole team was aware that the subject's health was in terminal decline, though no one ever said it out loud.

As Morris prepared the next exercise for Prisoner 501, Faulkner's words came into his mind.

'*Events may be moving beyond our control.*'

If the speculation about 501 was actually correct, then this whole research project might turn out to be an unprecedented disaster, and Morris's bid to resurrect his reputation as the brightest star among his peers, the final confirmation that he was over the hill and finished!

THIRTEEN

Arriving at the hut just after eight, Ray knocked lightly and heard a drawling voice telling him to enter. He stepped in and, although it was dark and cold outside, wanted to step right out again. Amidst the dismal light, smoke and stale smells, there was his uncle, in his crumpled suit, sitting in a deckchair cradling a plastic cup of whisky in his lap.

Well, the man's talent for interior design hasn't been lost on the hut, Ray thought, looking at the squalid chaos before him – *Skid Row at the seaside.* Ray felt spectacularly uncomfortable; the place was a dump, his uncle a mess and that sense of shame for, and shame of, the man felt almost overwhelming. Ray had always been a good Catholic boy and still retained one legacy of the faith in all its full, incapacitating glory: guilt and its derivative, shame. No one did shame and guilt better than Ray. He might be mediocre in every other aspect of his life, but he was outstanding at feeling self-contempt.

He still attended Mass with his insistent mother but of

late had begun to doubt many tenets of the faith. The fact that both his parents still upheld the Catholic doctrines added to his perpetual sense of confusion. For his father had broken one of its sacred vows, and his mother seemed intent on punishing him for it. Hardly the actions of 'Our Lord' as Ray understood them.

'Alright, boy,' his uncle mumbled as he tried to focus his eyes, and Ray recognised, with a sinking heart, the slightly slurred speech of a drunk.

God, this was even worse than his worst imaginings! Give the man the number and package and get out pronto!

'Do you know, boy, in just three short days my whole life's been turned to shit. Pardon my French,' Leary added, hiccupping.

Why did grown-ups always draw shocked attention to 'naughty' words you heard in the playground every day? Had they forgotten they'd heard and used them when they were kids? Ray wondered.

'I've got her phone number and a package,' said Ray. 'I… I can't stop long. Mum's due back soon. They've been giving her the extra hours she's been asking for.'

He passed across the paper and package. Leary groaned as he leaned forward in the deckchair to pick them up.

'Are you okay?' Ray asked.

'I've been better, boy. I have definitely been better. Somebody kicking… kicking the tripes out of you don't exactly leave you feeling like a kiddie in a fairground… Well, not unless it's Charlie Chuffin' Manley's!'

He widened his eyes as he attempted to focus on the package.

'You seen what's in this?' he asked suspiciously.

Ray faltered for a second while he thought about lying; but what was the point?

'Yeah,' he replied.

'Well, you shouldn't have! That was going to be my little bit of… security, see, for… Well… Anyway, that's all finished…'

There was an awkward silence and Ray prepared to make the little speech he had been rehearsing; like a low-calorie Judas about to betray a bargain-basement Jesus.

'Well, Uncle Garry,' he started, 'I think I should be—'

But his uncle had begun speaking at the same time. 'Listen, boy, I got plans to—'

They both stopped as the door handle behind Ray began to turn. Leary's red eyes blinked furiously in an attempt to sober up as he motioned his nephew to move around to his side of the table. The door was opening very, very gradually. He hauled himself clumsily up from his seat, looked around at the jumble of stuff behind him and picked out a baseball bat. He stood holding it, swaying slightly, the picnic table between him and the figure entering. Bowing its head under the low door frame it looked up, pushing the door closed behind it.

'Jeeez!' Leary exclaimed. 'You scared the bejingling bejabers out of me, you bloody idiot! I thought you was Manley and his boys again.'

Miss Zita Truman stood before them immobile, her face registering nothing.

Leary plonked back down in his chair, placed the bat across his knees, leisurely filled up his plastic cup again and looked the woman up and down slowly.

'But it ain't Porky and his pals, is it? It's… it's the elusive Zita!'

He gulped down the whisky and poured himself another shot. This woman had just destroyed any last ambitions in his crappy little life, and man, was he going to make her pay!

'Well, ain't this marvellous!' Leary began in mock-polite tones. 'Really good of you to find the time to visit us, Zita. 'Scuse the lodgings, won't you? Long story… Nah, short one, actually. See, I just lost me job, me office and me home… Funny, really, because I'm pretty certain I had 'em just before *you* popped round Monday, Zita. Now, where did I put 'em?' he asked, blearily looking down and patting his pockets.

'Oh, yeah,' he said, clicking his fingers, 'now I remember. They just upped and vanished. Ffffft! Like farts in a wind tunnel. Here! Same as you done, Zita!'

Zita Truman scanned the hut, momentarily focusing on Ray before returning her empty gaze to Leary's face.

'Still, all things considered, it ain't too bad really, is it?' Leary continued. 'Forty-two and living in a beach hut. I reckon it don't get much better really, does it?

'No, no. Hang on a mo. Now I think on, it does! See, I got a nice promise of alterna… alternative accommodation off Her Majesty, Zita. Nifty little ten… ten-be-five cell for a few years. I mean, who knows, if my luck with you holds, I might even have Charlie and his chums, what beat the crap out of me, sharing it. That'd be good, wouldn't it? We could play hide-and-seek in there. You know, like you done with me, Zita. Pass the time. Relieve the boredom like. Know what I mean?'

Zita Truman continued to look blankly at Leary.

'So. Hhhow you been keeping, me old duchess? Anybody kick *you* out of your home and work lately? Framed you? Beat the doodlies out of you? Take your time, Zita, 'cos there's no hurry.'

Miss Truman considered a moment. 'No. I am unsure about "frames" and "doodlies" … but no, I am quite well, thank you, Mr Leary.'

Ray was looking at Miss Truman's face with the sickly yellow pallor from the gas lantern on it. She was wearing her glasses again, so the intensity of her eyes was dulled, but there was something about the face that was odd, detached and disconcerting. He wondered if Miss Truman had had some kind of mental breakdown.

'Really? Well, isn't that super, Zita! Absolutely supaaaah!' Leary exclaimed. 'Big weight off me mind that is, knowing you're keeping well an' all… Still, I'm kind of wondering, though, if you can spare the time and it ain't too much trouble, if you got any clues why *my* life's just turned into something that clogs up toilets? You know, just to help us out a bit.'

Miss Truman stood a moment, processing the question before replying, 'No. No, I had no idea these forces would be unleashed upon you, Mr Leary. This is a very strange and dangerous place.'

'Really? So, app… apparently, I, ain't living in Santa's Merry Yuletide Grotto after all,' he said, waving his hand about the gloom and chaos of the hut.

'Mr Leary, are you being ironical? Mocking?' she asked, puzzled.

'What! Me mocking you, Zita? After all you done for me!'

'I am sorry for what has happened,' she said simply.

'Sorry?!' Leary exclaimed. 'Sorry... Well, how spiffin'! How absolutely spiffin' of you! Well, I reckon that makes it all alright again then, don't it, Zita? You're "sorry"! That's absolutely faffin' marvellous, that is! That'll make all the difference in court, that will, Zita – "the feminine touch".

'"Your honours," I'll say, "I'm homeless, unemployed, a drunk, a drug-pusher and I'm facing a few years in the nick. But you know what... Hic... Miss Kim Kardashian here says she's verrah, verrah sorrah for it all!"

'"Really?" they'll say. "Well, in that case, old boy, not only are all charges dropped, but we'd just love it if you could pop round to our gaff for a bit of tea and tiffin. Oh, and don't you forget to bring your gormless, brain-dead, pug-ugly pal there with you!"'

It passed through Ray's mind that Uncle Garry's drunken, cocky aggression might have been increased by the fact that Miss Truman appeared to be the meekest, least threatening and pompous adult he'd ever met. His uncle was behaving really, really badly.

'Uncle Garry—' he began.

'And you can shut it before you start, boy! This flamin' oddball has screwed my life up and then left me in the bloody lurch to face the music. So, you keep it shut, right?!'

Leary's mood was changing to very sour as he waved a warning, drifting finger at his nephew.

'Mr Leary, that is the most discourteous behaviour,' Miss Truman observed.

'Listen, love, if I want the monkey there to talk, I'll rattle a bag of nuts for it. See?'

'Rattle a bag of—?' Miss Truman broke off, spotting the bottle of whisky.

'Ah! Self-medication,' she continued quietly. 'Now, that would explain it.'

'Self-medi—? What you talkin' about?' Leary demanded, confused.

'Simply, that I have observed that alcohol, drugs, food, or whatever is at hand, is frequently employed to medicate, comfort, soothe or support oneself. It appears to assist in facing the many challenges life here poses, though its impact on clarity of thinking can be immense, as I am witnessing now. One begins to speculate that, perhaps, mind or emotion-state-altering drugs are essential to maintain sanity and stability here. This whole area is really most intriguing… Now, what of the investigation? What is its progress?'

'You what?'

Leary's mood was shifting from rambling, sarcastic drunk to cold, calculating viciousness.

'I asked you, Mr Leary, what you have learnt about my brother from your investigation.'

'Did you? Did you really?'

'Yes.'

Leary seemed to suddenly sober up. He stood up, brandishing the baseball bat.

'Do you know something, lady?' he said quietly, leaning towards her. 'I'm just about holding meself back from belting you one.'

'Ah, yes. Violence,' Miss Truman said as flatly as before. 'The usual frustrated response to any difficulty deemed too challenging.'

'What?!' Leary asked, genuinely outraged, confused and flabbergasted by the woman's apparent lack of response to his aggression. She seemed not only unintimidated but kind of uninterested as well.

'Mr Leary, I require information from you regarding the progress of your investigation. I have given you a very substantial deposit for the work so far. I have apologised for the troubles it has brought on you, but now I really must insist that you tell me where my brother is currently located, and what has happened to him.'

'Listen, lady, you don't insist on nothing! Right? When I'm running a case, I...' Leary's alcohol-fumed brain struggled to find a sufficiently forceful expression but failed. 'Run it! Right? Me! Not you! Me!'

'Mr Leary, I am asking you to calm yourself, please. Your behaviour and manners are really quite disturbing, particularly for the person here,' she said gently, indicating Ray.

'You telling me how to behave now, Zita?! 'Cos I'm telling you, if the boy there don't like it,' Leary nodded at Ray, 'he can sling his hook anytime he wants, see!'

'Really, this is most unpleasant to witness, Mr Leary. You are so very disrespectful in your manner towards him.'

'What?! Are you for bloody real, missus? It may have escaped your notice, love, but I'm facing five years in the nick, Zita! Five years! So, if I'm not "respectful" to the boy there, I couldn't actually give one! Right?!'

'I must apologise for this man's behaviour,' Miss Truman said, turning to Ray. 'I believe I may have inadvertently irritated him; a combination of his hormones and alcohol are getting the better of his cognition, and now, because he doubts his ability to challenge me on an intellectual level, he is wrongfully expressing his anger towards you. It is a rather clichéd scenario I see so very often.'

'Don't… Hic… Don't you bloody apologise for me, darling! That boy's here out the goodness of my heart, see,' Leary said, his eyes blazing.

'Oh, Mr Leary, I really, really do despair of you. Will you please cease the puerile behaviour, treat this individual with the respect he deserves and give me the information for which I traded the diamonds.'

'Puerile? What's that mean? Nah! Nah! Don't bother explaining, love, 'cos you're getting nowt out of me! Right? Nothing! Diddly, diddly squat!'

Ray, ashamed and hurt by Leary's words, spoke quietly but clearly. 'The police took him from a flat in Barton Road.'

Leary turned with fury towards the lad.

'I told you to keep your bloody mouth shut, boy!' he said viciously. 'You say one more thing and I'm—'

Miss Truman raised her hand authoritatively at Leary to silence him. Stepping up to Ray, she looked long and hard into his face as if seeing it for the first time, carefully studying each eye, curve and feature.

'Your name is Raymond, is it not? Thank you, Raymond, for your empathy and kindness,' she finally said. 'These are much rarer commodities than I had ever anticipated,' and she tilted her head as if appraising Ray yet again.

Then she turned to his uncle. 'Mr Leary, I have observed that you do not treat Raymond with anything like the courtesy he warrants. However, that is between the two of you and I have no right to interfere. But I will not stand by and see him insulted with outright contempt. That is quite unacceptable. Do you understand me?'

Leary was confused and disorientated. He felt as if he had just been well and truly told off. And he didn't like it one bit!

She continued, 'I cannot do this on my own. I require just two more things from you. I will pay you additional sums if necessary.'

Leary felt oddly relieved by the change in direction the conversation had taken. He'd been totally stunned and sobered up by the boy's interruption. He'd been telling the kid to stand up for himself and be more of a man, but he'd certainly not expected something like that of him!

'Listen, lady!' he said to her. 'I ain't got a clue what's going on here but, whatever it is has seriously cocked up my life. Do you get that? Now, you're going to tell me a whole lot more, and it's going cost you—'

'I will give you five more diamonds,' she stated crisply.

Leary was stopped in his tracks. Five more diamonds plus the two he already had at £10,000 to £15,000 a gem… were serious, serious money! A whole new life for Lorraine and the boy had suddenly opened up before him!

'What do you want?' Leary asked suspiciously.

'I want you to find where my brother is being held and accompany me on a visit to him.' She paused, then continued, 'I would like Raymond's company also.'

'Oh no, you don't! Nah! Nah! The… Raymond's underage. I wouldn't do that without his mum's say-so, and she ain't going to give it, see.'

'May we ask Raymond himself?' Miss Truman suggested.

'I'd like to help,' Ray cut in quickly.

Leary's head was spinning. This woman held out the prospect for a whole new life for them all. He also sensed he would have to work at rebuilding whatever it was that had first attracted his nephew to visit him.

'Thank you, Raymond,' Zita Truman said simply. 'Mr Leary?'

Leary had taken out a notebook and was pretending to leaf through it.

'Will you do this?'

'Listen… Listen, I'll find out what I can and decide about the rest later, see,' Leary finally said.

'We will meet again here tomorrow night at the same time. This is acceptable to you?' Miss Truman asked.

Leary nodded. She looked carefully at him, then Ray, turned and left the hut.

'Sorry… for speaking out like that,' Ray ventured after a long silence.

'Yeah. Right. Well, don't do it again, see,' Leary said, shifting uneasily and still not meeting his eye. 'You'd better get off home 'fore your mum gets back.'

'Thanks,' Ray said and left.

Leary picked up the whisky bottle, looked at it a moment before putting it down again. His thumping head needed to be much, much clearer.

*

Ray got back in plenty of time and was upstairs, apparently doing his Design Technology project, when his mother looked in on him. She'd been in a really good mood and, though tired, was delighted with the extra money the next ten days' overtime would bring in. Her manager had been lovely with her ever since that awful interview. Apparently, she'd said that Mrs Bradnock had a very promising future with the company.

Then she had turned in, telling him not to work beyond eleven. She said before she left how pleased she was with his change of attitude.

Ray put the work aside as soon as she'd gone and went back to reviewing the events of the evening. He felt weird. Absolutely weird. But great as well! It was just so fantastic to have someone on his side for a change! He'd really admired Miss Truman for what she'd said on his behalf.

He'd listened to his mother talking about her boss and suspected she was being rewarded for 'sorting out her son'. It made him feel odd, a bit guilty, but also protective towards her. Because, for once in his life, he seemed to have a lot more of a clue about what was going on than she did.

FOURTEEN

Leary met up the following Friday afternoon with Detective Sergeant William Clarkson for a pint at the Duke of Gloucester in Exeter. He and Billy had been good mates in their army days. He'd covered for Billy when their scam in Germany had gone belly-up. He didn't consider it any kind of noble act on his part; you just didn't drop your 'oppos' in it. He'd asked Billy to make some discreet enquiries about the Truman brother's arrest and disappearance.

When they sat down at a table, he'd seen how preoccupied Billy appeared. With none of the usual banter, Clarkson spoke quietly and earnestly. Having looked into the case, he'd discovered that Truman's brother was a special 'Category F' prisoner, which covered offences ranging from espionage to terrorism. He could be held for trial indefinitely while investigations proceeded, had no right to legal representation and could be sent to wherever the country's security forces determined. He was currently being held at the Royal Commando base at Derringham.

'The whole thing's weird really,' he concluded, ''cos to all intents and purposes this bloke doesn't exist anymore. You want my advice? Just walk away. You got enough on your plate as it is,' Clarkson had advised him.

When Leary had pressed for further information Clarkson had turned quite aggressive, for him. 'Listen, the chiefs on the top floor, they ever get wind I've told you this, I'm out on me ear! It's a sackable offence, see.'

'Aw, come on, Billy,' Leary had joshed. 'Shooting the breeze with an old army mucker, a sackable offence? What is it? Full court-martial and your truncheon broke over your helmet, for a tip on the gee-gees?'

'You really think this is some kind of bloody joke, don't you, Garry? I'm telling you, you want to grow up, man. You're not getting it, are you? This isn't a couple of squaddies messing round with fags and booze contraband. This is a major global terrorist we're talking about, and that's highly classified information I've just given you.'

He leaned forward, glancing from side to side at the pub's regulars and hissed, 'I could be banged up for what I've just told you, so listen. When my chief super calls me into his office on the top floor, demanding to know what I'm doing with a bloke on drugs charges as a pal, I can see my career and pension disappearing fast.

'You were a good mate to me, Garry, all those years back, but don't push it. What I've just given you makes us equals, see? I don't owe you nothing. You don't, me. Okay? If we happen to meet down the Legion that's fine, but there's no more stuff like this, right? Now, I'm telling you for the last time, stay as far away from this feller as you can!'

Leary had been surprised by Clarkson's irritable nervousness throughout the conversation. More than that, though, he recognised how uneasy he felt himself. As he'd walked through the city centre, he had been aware, for the first time, of just how many CCTV cameras there were around the place.

He had also felt as if he was being followed. He didn't know if it was some kind of sixth sense, or just his paranoia in overdrive. Whatever it was, he wanted out of this case. Pronto!

*

'Right. Who's this copper, Clarkson?' Manley demanded of Warrington.

'I told you, Charlie. He was in the army with Leary. Rumour is he was involved in that smuggling stuff in Berlin Leary got kicked out for.'

'A copper smuggling? Hmm. Might come in handy later. What were they talking about, then?'

Jonas Warrington was standing in front of his brother-in-law's desk like a very tall naughty schoolboy before a squat headteacher. Manley had a thing about his short stature, so Warrington's six-foot-three presence alone seemed enough to bring out the worst in the man. Manley had always treated him with little in the way of respect but was becoming much worse since linking up with Gerald Dunstable.

'How would I know, Charlie? I was standing across the street from the pub!'

'Here, you watch your tone. Right?' Manley warned. 'So why weren't you in the place?'

'Come on, Charlie! It was hard enough following Leary without him catching on.'

'Yeah? Maybe we're not paying you enough, Jonas. Is that it? Couple of grand being thrown your way for a bit of leg-work.'

'No, Charlie! Me and Shirley's grateful for the stuff you're putting my way, but the pub had no place to hide a man my size in.'

'Perhaps if your legs went missing.'

'What's that mean, Charlie?!' Warrington demanded, shocked and puzzled.

Shirley was nothing like her brother, Warrington contemplated again. He was a nasty piece and getting nastier by the day. Warrington had only taken on Manley's work because his private investigation business was struggling. Having Leary arrive as a competitor in the town was the last thing he'd needed.

'Nothing,' Manley replied. 'Just thinking aloud… You do know that Gerry Dunstable's likely to be a very, very wealthy man. We're talking millions, right? He's putting a lot of work my way, Jonas, so he's got a right to expect better stuff than this. You getting squeamish again?'

'Listen, Charlie, my business is legitimate,' Warrington protested.

'Oh, yeah! That's why you got my only sister living in a two-bedroom terrace, and I've just put the deposit down on a five-acre spread out in Salcombe. Shirl's got a heart of gold, and a brain that's dense as lead, see. You ain't the provider I had in mind for her, Jonas. So up your game, will you?'

'I'm not breaking the law, Charlie!'

'Didn't ask you to. You got scruples about what happened to Leary. Fine by me. Keep looking the other way. But Leary's a serious cockroach in Gerry's soufflé, see. That little toe rag should've been back in Hackney, under the rock he crawled out of by now. As for scruples, they're for people what can afford 'em, Jonas. And you ain't in that bracket yet, boy. Not by a long chalk.

'Gerry ain't too impressed with you neither,' he continued, 'gawping while Leary's taking the right royal rip out of him. I could have brought a rottin', bloody corpse to that meeting and got a better performance out of it than you give! Stood there, drooping like six foot-odd of chicken piss!'

Suddenly angered, he got up from behind his desk, moved ponderously around it and stood, inches from his brother-in-law, looking up into his face.

He spoke very quietly. 'If Gerry Dunstable decides he can get better service elsewhere and breaks up this lucrative partnership, guess who I'm going to be blaming, Jonas?'

Warrington looked away.

'It ain't hard. I'm a real easy man to get along with. Really, you ask anyone. I don't ask much. I looks out for me family and I takes care of 'em. I also takes care of those that don't take care of 'em. Sounds confusing that, don't it? You following me, Jonas?'

'Yeah,' Warrington muttered.

'Can't hear you.'

'Yes.'

'Oh good. You let Leary give you the slip and, getting back to that leg business you didn't understand earlier, I'll take you down a couple of foot. Permanently. Brother-in-law or not! See?'

FIFTEEN

That evening Leary and Ray were sitting on deckchairs in the hut awaiting Miss Truman. Apart from acknowledging each other, the two had remained in silence. For the first time Ray had not felt any awkwardness or the need to make conversation; as if he didn't have to try so hard.

At exactly 8.30pm Zita Truman had arrived and a farcical scene had ensued. She'd sat down, as requested by Leary, in the metal-framed beach chair facing the pair of them, and it had collapsed beneath her. She'd looked ridiculous, her legs in the air and the back of her beret-covered head clunking loudly on the wooden floor.

They'd gone to assist her, but she'd held up her hand to prevent it. As she got up, she hadn't looked hurt or even vaguely embarrassed, but had stood while Leary told her what he had learnt.

At the conclusion Leary said, 'So that's about it, lady. You got what you want. Now, where's my part of the deal?'

'I still have my last request, Mr Leary. To see where my brother is incarcerated.'

Leary narrowed his eyes and looked suspiciously at her. 'What the hell for? I've just told you where he is. Listen, if you think they're going let you in a high-security army barracks, so you can shoot the breeze with your psycho brother, you're even more off your chump than you look. Anyway, how come he ain't been asking to see you?'

'Mr Leary, my brother and I have been separated for some time. I just wish to see where he is located. It would be a kindness if you would accompany me.'

'Yeah, well, sorry, love, but I ain't in the kindness business, see,' Leary replied.

'I would pay you very handsomely for such a service, Mr Leary, and that would be our business concluded,' she said.

'Hang on. Let me get this straight. You're offering me a small fortune for just seeing where they're holding him. Yeah? So, what's going on, Zita? What's the deal? You some kind of eccentric bleedin' lottery winner, 'cos this lot don't add up? That diamond my mate said was one of the finest stones he's ever seen.'

'I am an individual of, shall we say, considerable resources, Mr Leary. You yourself impressed upon me when we first met that you did not require too much information of a personal nature from me.'

'Yeah', said Leary, 'that's before your bro turned out to be a little spicy cocktail of Jacky Ripper and Ossie Bin Laden.'

'I am asking for this one last service, Mr Leary… And, of course, if Raymond will also accompany us there.'

Leary shook his head furiously. 'Nah, nah, nah, nah, nah! No way, lady! I didn't say nothing about taking the boy Raymond along.'

'Ah, come on, Uncle Garry,' Ray cut in, 'Mum doesn't need to know about any of this. Where's the harm in just driving there and looking?'

Miss Truman drew Leary to one side and, dipping in her handbag, drew out a handful of something Ray could identify by the clinking sound were more diamonds. Leary looked startled. He stood a moment weighing things up, then sighed and shook his head.

'Alright… Alright, lady. You got a deal. We go there, we look, and we leave. And you give me everything you just shown me. Right? And I mean everything. Then you and me are done.'

Miss Truman nodded. 'Of course.'

He turned to Ray. 'And as for you, boy, if I'm about to stick me knackers in the proverbial juicer, you'd better be bloody sure you do exactly what I tell you, right? That means you get to come on two conditions, see. One: you keep your face shut while we're there. And two: you keep it doubly shut when we get back. Right?'

'Mr Leary, that is not at all respectful,' Miss Truman observed.

Leary felt confused and angry again. 'Look, lady, how I talk to the boy there is my business, right? You said so yourself, didn't you? I'm responsible for him, see.'

'Is it not possible to feel responsible for him and respectful of him at the same time? I would have thought there was a high level of correlation between the two attitudes.'

'What?! Look, lady, with all due… respect, you don't know what's going on here, do you? The boy's mum don't want him involved with me, right? And I respect that, see.'

'Ah! So, as I understand it, you respect the mother's viewpoint but not her son's, even though she has rejected you whilst he is trying his best to be helpful to us both. Confusing. However, I leave you to resolve that particular dilemma for yourself.'

Leary's brain was spinning again. Part of him was absolutely furious with her and another part, the annoying bit, was feeling something akin to shame. There was a moment's silence as he tried to get himself back in charge of the situation again, but Zita Truman spoke first.

'So, we are to meet tomorrow. I will have a vehicle. When and where will the meeting be exactly?'

'Make it the railway car park at nine. And you make sure you bring all them with you, right?' He pointed at Miss Truman's handbag.

'Thank you, Mr Leary. I very much appreciate this,' she said simply and then left.

He looked hard at Ray. 'I'm in big trouble with your ma if she ever finds out about this. Right? She'd ban me for life from ever having anything more to do with the pair of you. You get that, don't you? I'm going to be trusting you like I never trusted anyone before. Don't you let me down, boy!'

'I won't. And thanks a lot, Uncle Garry.'

Leary inspected the crumpled beach chair. 'That's the living room furniture beggared then,' he muttered. 'Well, go on,' he said to Ray irritably, 'get yourself off home.'

Ray stepped out and smiled to himself; finally, something was going his way!

SIXTEEN

It was a wet, cold Saturday morning outside Building 7 at the Derringham Commando Training Barracks as Professor Morris, his hand chafing his chin red, looked again at the readings from last night's research session. Nothing. No indications of any abnormalities at all. Five months he and his team had been working on this project and they had virtually zero to report.

Perhaps the whole damned thing really was just some elaborate hoax! And yet, as Faulkner had reminded him again, there was that mechanism they had taken from the subject's flat. It had traces of an unusual wavelength of radioactive material. A separate team was engaged in researching it and making the same woefully feeble progress he was.

The rumours circulating for the last couple of months that Morris's services to the project would shortly be dispensed with, and a new 'genius' assigned as project leader, had been confirmed by Faulkner's visit. That was why he had allowed his desperation and ambition to overtake any sense of ethics. For Prisoner 501 was dying; no doubt about that. No matter what nutrients they forced or dripped into him, his body's functions were in terminal decline.

Once, accidentally, Morris had come across the photographs they had taken of the subject when he was first seized; a kindly, gentle, confused expression had looked back at him. He contrasted that with the emaciated, tortured-looking figure he had left an hour ago. It reminded him uncomfortably of those scarecrows who had emerged from death camps.

He shook himself. Death camps! Sheer, cheap sensationalism! There was no comparison between what his team did and the actions of those acting on behalf of criminal dictators! That figure in the orange overall represented a serious threat to national security! If he wasn't what they suspected, why hadn't he opened his mouth just once to deny it?

'Professor Morris? Major General Phillips would like a word,' Jeremy Brint informed him, standing at the doorway, the hint of a smile lingering around his mouth.

'What the hell does he want now?' Morris asked, months of exasperation with the military's constant nosiness erupting.

It always tickled Brint to see 'Mr Prodigy' lose all that glacial self-control.

'He's out in reception. Says he's not leaving till he's spoken to you,' Brint added helpfully.

'Really? Have you seen these latest readings, Brint?' Morris asked viciously. 'This set here? They could be out by a factor of twenty. I suggest you get them recalibrated. Immediately. Have them on my desk in ten minutes.

'Oh, and in case you hadn't noticed,' he added, 'all our reputations and livelihoods are currently on the line. You've probably heard rumours of my early expulsion from this project, Brint, so let me reassure you about something. If I'm going, so is every last man-jack of you. Let me also point out that any reference for employment you subsequently require is unlikely to qualify you for either Starbucks, Costa or Wetherspoons!

'Interesting. I see you're not smirking now,' he concluded.

Brint, flustered and annoyed, took himself off. Perhaps he and the rest of the team would have performed better if they knew what the hell it was they were meant to be researching!

SEVENTEEN

It was miserable, wet, cold and the end of Ray's first week's holiday when he arrived at the railway station, having done his paper round and left his bike at the shop. He was due to go up to Birmingham from this station the following Monday.

And he was dreading it!

He was all too aware that he would have to try to fit in with his father's new household and pretend he didn't resent his partner, Jasmine. He had met her just once before. She was alright, but she seemed as awkward with him as he was with her. He also didn't know what he would make of the new baby sister, Harper, he'd just acquired.

He arrived, surprised to find Miss Truman sitting behind the wheel of an Enterprise van, delivered earlier, with the driver's side suspension noticeably down. He would never have associated this tall, refined spinster with 'White Van Man'.

She greeted him in her usual calm and detached manner, and the two sat watching the rain bounce off the windscreen. Normally Ray was awkward about sitting with an adult in silence, feeling pressure to fill the void, but he felt perfectly comfortable with her; accepted and equal somehow. Leary had arrived later looking irritable. Ray recognised the mood and drew as little attention to himself as possible.

He sat between the two adults as Miss Truman started up the van, revved it loudly, let out the clutch and stalled it with a violent lurch forward. She twisted the ignition key, Leary muttering, and 'kangarooed' the van a couple of yards further before it stalled again.

'Jesus!' Leary muttered, shaking his head in disbelief.

She started it up again, the engine howling as her foot pressed the accelerator pedal to the floor. The clutch went out and the van lurched to another full stop, Ray and his uncle being thrown forward.

'Jesus!' Leary repeated. 'We'll be here all flippin' day at this rate, love! How about letting me do the driving?'

'I am unfamiliar with the hydraulic pressure required to engage the clutch with the gear mechanism. Perhaps it would be for the best,' she replied, taking off the seat belt.

'Yeah… Right.'

The driver's side suspension rose as Miss Truman got out, and depressed on the passenger's side as she climbed back in. Ray became aware of a real sense of weight beside him. Well, Miss Truman was quite a tall woman, Ray thought. Perhaps she was 'big-boned' as his mother described heavy people.

Ray kept his mouth tight shut and looked studiously out the windscreen as Leary muttered and cussed to himself.

'What d'you get a van for anyway?' he asked the woman belligerently.

He didn't bother awaiting a reply but continued to mutter, 'Waste of bloody time… Don't know how I get into these faffin' messes… When I think of all…'

And so on and so forth. Ray had seen kids get seriously 'done' for such a sulky carry-on, but once again in the world of grown-ups, it was, 'Do as I say, not as I do', apparently. Wasn't that a further example of Uncle Garry's own 'prestidigitation'?

As the vehicle laboured up another hill, Leary snorted with derision. 'Can't get any poke out the beggar. What you got in the back of it, Zita? Couple of anvils and a boulder?'

'No. I will examine the engine when we stop,' Miss Truman replied, continuing to look straight ahead of her.

'Ah, no need to trouble yourself with that stuff, love. You'll only get yourself all mussed up. I'll take a little shufti at it for you,' Leary replied gallantly.

'Indeed,' Miss Truman said. 'Tell me, Mr Leary, are you fully conversant with the dynamic processes of the four-cylinder, fuel-injected, three-point-two-litre diesel engine?'

'What?'

'Well, fortunately I am,' she said flatly.

Leary rolled his eyes and lapsed into silence. What a weird, bloody woman, he thought again; one of them, what was it they called them? Oh yeah! Blue-stocking types! All brains and no personality or looks! She was already seriously getting on his thruppenny bits!

The wind and rain continued to buffet the sides of the van whenever they came out of the cover of houses and trees. Ray felt a momentary surge of guilt when he considered just how far he was going against his mother's express wishes, but he was learning to shrug it off quicker. He *was* deceiving her. He'd told her he was going out with some imaginary mates, and she'd seemed pleased, which made it even worse.

He really, really wished he didn't have to lie but she didn't seem to leave him much option. He was doing what he wanted, as opposed to what she wanted. And, well, if that wasn't growing up and taking more responsibility for himself, he didn't know what was.

'Some beggar's tailing us,' Leary suddenly said.

He turned off down a side road and the silver-grey car reappeared some 200 metres behind them when they entered a straight stretch.

'Yep. Definitely following. I'd stake big money that's Warrington's car. Well, I can't outrun it in this heap of junk.'

He turned down another narrow Devon country lane where there was little space on either side between the van and overhanging hedges. Driving on till he found a sharp bend with an entrance into a field, he travelled just past it and pulled up.

Telling the others to stay put and cursing the wet, he moved down the side of the vehicle to the field's entrance. He pulled up a thick piece of turf, hunted around and found a stick. Staying out of sight, he waited for the car to appear and stop behind the van. As it came to a halt, he followed it up and stood behind with the turf and stick clearly visible. He banged on the boot lid and Warrington stuck his head out of the window and looked backwards, confused, at him.

'Here, Warrington! You make one move and I'm bunging this up your exhaust and ramming it well up with this stick. And you won't be going anywhere for a long time, pal. Now, what's the idea?'

'Jesus, Leary!' Warrington said angrily. 'What the hell are you playing at?'

'I'll tell you what I'm playing at, pal. I'm getting wet, tired and pissed off and I'm doing it now, see.'

Leary bent down to reach the exhaust pipe.

'Alright! Alright! I'll tell you!' Warrington shouted. 'Charlie's told me to follow you.'

'Charlie! Charlie Piggin' Manley! Jeez! How do you sleep nights, Warrington? Your arse of a brother-in-law and that poncey pal of his have carved my life up. I always had you down as a daft beggar. I never pegged you as a mean sod.'

Warrington looked confused and troubled. 'I'm not happy with what they've done to you, Leary! I didn't know what they had planned. He's… he's me brother-in-law.'

'Oh, Jesus!' Leary said sarcastically. 'So that puts you in the clear, does it, 'cos you're just following orders what the wife's brother give you. You're a tripeless bloody wonder, aren't you, Warrington?'

'Listen, Leary, after I've done this, I'm planning to get out of Brookdale. Start up somewhere else away from him. Shirley doesn't like what he's doing any more than I do. I don't expect you to believe me, but it's the truth!'

Leary looked at him intently. 'Yeah? So, what?' he asked finally.

'So, how about letting me follow you?' Warrington suggested doubtfully.

'Oh, yeah? And why would I do that?' Leary asked.

''Cos if I lose you, I'm in big trouble. Charlie's going to give me the same treatment you got!' Warrington replied.

'And why should that bother me, Warrington? You got it coming.'

''Cos I haven't got it coming and you know it! I haven't done anything to you, Leary! Once I've done this, I'm off the case! What difference does it make if I follow this once? How about it? Just follow? I'd be out your hair for good after that. You'd have the whole town to yourself! I swear!'

Warrington sounded desperate. Leary considered.

'Alright,' he said finally, 'but this is how it's goin' to work, see, Warrington. Far as you're concerned, I'm Field Marshall Frickin' Leary on this little "military expedition" and you're just the poor muckin' grunt who joined up yesterday. Get the picture. I'm running the show, see? You don't break wind without my say-so, and I say how loud and where you point your backside, right? Now, we're leaving your car in Templeford, see, and you're getting in the van.'

'Bloody hell, Leary! You're laying it on a bit thick, aren't you?' Warrington cried.

'Okay, Jonas. You throw your lot in with good old Charlie, then. Just let me know what the coma's like if you ever wake up from it.'

He began to bend towards the car's exhaust.

'Alright! Alright!' Warrington shouted.

''Bout bloody time! I'm getting soaked standing here and you owe me for the rest of your natural life, see?'

'Okay! Okay! I get it! I just don't want any tricks, Leary!' Warrington demanded.

Twenty minutes later Leary pulled up at the car park of The Admiral public house in Templeford. After perfunctory greetings, with Warrington glaring at Miss Truman for not paying him for the work he had done on her behalf, he climbed into the back and sat on some dust sheets, his knees drawn up to his chin.

He looked not very happy with the arrangement. He had suggested the 'kid' might be better in the back, and Ray had been delighted with Uncle Garry's response, even if it wasn't quite the absolute truth.

'He's invited, Warrington. You're a gate-crasher. Get in the back.'

EIGHTEEN

Gerald Dunstable was looking far from his usual, unflappable self today Manley noted; no offer of a drink this morning!

'So, as I say, certain... issues may be coming to something of a head,' Dunstable concluded, his brow uncharacteristically furrowed. 'Please excuse my fatigue but we had a little emergency here last night.'

Manley wondered if it referred to that weird beggar, Vader. He'd never actually met Ian Vader in all the time he'd been working for Gerald Dunstable. He was supposed to be some kind of eccentric, genius-recluse like that Howard Hughes nutter. Just once Manley had caught sight of Vader's back when he had arrived, unannounced, with further news about Leary. The other man had fairly scuttled out of the place.

'Oh yeah?' Manley asked.

'Nothing to concern yourself about, Charles. You're sure Warrington's up to this?' Dunstable asked Manley again, to change the subject.

'Oh definitely. We had a little chat a couple of days back and I straightened him out, Gerry. He knows exactly what side his bread's buttered on.'

'You can't go in there yet, Mrs Welch—' Jenny's voice rang out in reception.

'Nonsense, Jenny! Mr Dunstable said he wanted to be updated immediately.'

Margaret Welch, Vader's personal nurse, bustled through, all smiles, glasses, floral patterns and large handbag. Dunstable was furious. The overarching strategy of all he did with regard to Vader was to keep each individual separated from the other, with himself as the centre of control between them all.

'Alright, love,' Manley greeted her.

'Oh! Mr Manley! How very surprising to see *you* here.'

'We met before, love?' Manley asked her, puzzled.

'No. But you are well known in the town,' she replied, smiling graciously.

Dunstable knew her well enough by now to recognise disapproval in her tone and look.

'Ian's sleeping now, Gerald,' she lisped. 'I really do think that was the worst episode he's had yet.' She turned to the other man to engage him in the conversation. 'He was very, very distressed, Mr Manley.'

'How's that?' Manley asked, puzzled.

'Ian… Mr Vader has these little turns sometimes. Nightmares. Very sensitive, you understand.' She adopted a concerned expression to convey her compassionate devotion to the man.

Manley might have been able to understand many things, Dunstable thought, but sensitivity certainly wasn't one of them! If news of Vader's mental instability ever got out, it could wipe millions off the company's potential share value!

'Yes, I wonder if we can leave this until later, Margaret?' Dunstable suggested. 'I just have this business to conclude with Mr Manley first. We're discussing some new land out at the factory.'

'Of course, Mr Dunstable. I've had to up Ian's medication, by the way, but he is so looking forward to his party tonight,' she added brightly.

Good God! Can't the stupid madam recognise a hint to keep it shut? Dunstable thought.

'Party?' Manley asked suspiciously.

'Yes, it's… it's just a small affair for some of Ian's particularly close friends,' Dunstable said dismissively.

A recluse with close friends? That's a first, Manley thought.

Suddenly he was feeling a little raw and sensitive himself. If there was a party tonight, why hadn't he been invited? Not good enough, or what? Dunstable had simply told him to be around the Vader headquarters in case something happened.

'Ian's still very, very on the edge. Are you absolutely certain you don't want me there, Gerald?' the nurse asked him.

The bottom of a deep ditch with a liberal sprinkling of lime over her was Dunstable's preferred destination for Margaret Welch at that particular moment.

'No, thank you, Margaret. Take the night off. You've earned it.' He smiled and winked charmingly at her.

In Dunstable's mind, Margaret Welch had just slotted in nicely between Ian Vader and Charles Manley in the 'dumping' schedule he updated daily.

NINETEEN

Leary and Warrington had decided not to approach Derringham Commando Training Barracks directly, but to park up on higher ground overlooking it, some 800 metres away. Warrington's time there as a marine was proving useful as he directed them.

They turned into a field, kept close to the hedges, and made bumpy progress around it to a spot overlooking the base. Leary, ready for a quick departure, if necessary, parked the van with the back facing the hedge and the front pointing towards the entrance to the field.

Zita Truman, uncharacteristically, had seemed to become agitated and tense. She sat for a minute or two, deep in thought. Then she got out, with Warrington assisting, lifted the bonnet of the van and inspected the engine while Leary rolled a cigarette.

Warrington walked up to the hedge and looked down at the base through the binoculars Leary had brought. Ray stood next to him, shivering. The rain had temporarily stopped, but a biting wind still blew. Warrington passed the binoculars across to the lad.

The base looked eerily deserted and bland. A five-metre-high, electrified fence ran around it, with surveillance cameras posted every fifty metres along the perimeter. At the entrance were two red and white barriers and between them, a round, stone guardhouse. There were various anonymous-looking blocks dotted behind it and a car park full of white vans and civilian vehicles. It looked more like a university campus than a military installation.

Leary, standing with his back to Truman, put his cigarette in his mouth while he rubbed his hands together to get some feeling back in them. He walked across to Warrington who was staring intently at the base, having reclaimed the binoculars. He passed them back to Ray, ready for a bit of a chat, even if it was with Leary!

'Funny being back,' Warrington observed. 'First time in ages. Good times an' all. Tough, though. No room for the weak or squeamish here. You were infantry, weren't you, Leary?' Warrington asked, with a little superiority in the tone.

It was common practice for anyone who'd undergone the rigours of commando training to disparage those who hadn't.

'Yep. Devonshire. Hated it,' Leary replied brusquely.

He knew the game and wasn't about to play it.

'What did you join up for, then?' Warrington asked.

'My old man took me along to the recruitment centre. Signed me up for sixteen years. Drunken old sot!'

'You didn't have to go.'

'That or juvenile prison, see.'

'You a bad 'un?' Warrington asked.

'You name it, I was into it.'

'So… er… so what did they throw you out for?' Warrington asked, tentatively.

'Not that it's any of your business, Pinocchio, but a couple of mates and me had a bit of a racket going on in Berlin. Just spirits, fags and baccy. My idea, see, I'm fronting it, so I took the rap. One of my oppos suitably grateful. Never heard from the other arse when I got out. Someone told me he made it to non-commissioned officer… Well, that figures. See, what we didn't know was a few cases of the commanding officer's special vintage Napoleon brandy somehow got in the mix. Vindictive old basket he was.

'"You're an absolute disgrace to the honour of the uniform you wear, Leary! A total, absolute shower!" he bawls at me in his office.'

'Yeah, well, it's a good life in the military if you stick by the rules,' Warrington observed tartly. 'They take good care of you. Keep you out of trouble.'

'Oh yeah!' Leary replied. 'Three square meals a day and a bit of cash in your back pocket. All you got to do is shoot the occasional beggar now and then. Or get shot and lose the odd arm, leg or bollock… Definitely keeps you out of trouble, though!'

'Defending your country!' Warrington said, becoming annoyed.

'Oh yeah? Which one? Yours, mine, or Dunstable's?' Leary asked.

'Same difference! We're all in the same boat!' Warrington countered.

'That why you and me is freezing our cobblers off in

a field and Dunstable's sitting in a posh office, toasting his on the underfloor heating?

'Same boat! Jesus! You want to grow up, Warrington! Same piggin' boat! You and me is deep down in the galleys, boy, rowing like silly beggars in case you hadn't noticed. Dunstable and his sort's up top, sunning themselves and bashing the tub quicker when they fancy a bit of water-skiing.'

'Ruddy communist stuff that, Leary!' Warrington declared, disgusted.

'Jeez! Same old guff. You mention a bit of fairness and suddenly you're Karl Muckin' Marx! You ever actually read *Das Kapital*, Warrington? One of Karl's bedtime readers. Gorgeous German piece, Ingrid Schmidt, introduced it to me when I was stationed out in Berlin. Place was full of radicals back then, all trying to convert you to the cause. Schmidt probably wasn't even her real name.

'She'd been banging on about it for months. Looked like she was getting fed up with us, so I give it a go, see. Provide a bit of pillow talk, like. Couldn't put it down! Like I'd been sleepwalking all me life.

'I'm telling you, I'm no bloody commie, Warrington, though the chuffin' authorities thought I was... Yeah, I paid big time for a few rolls in the hay with old Ingrid.

'"Consorting with undesirables", apparently. "Conduct unbecoming et cetera, et cetera." What with that and the scam, they threw the bleedin' book, the library and the easy chairs at me! Two years in the Glasshouse for a measly two and a half grand split three ways... Fact was, I just didn't want to be a mug anymore!'

There was an awkward, angry silence between them.

'What we doing here?' Warrington finally asked, to change the subject.

'Search me,' said Leary. '"Zita" wanted a visit. She's paying, so I brought her.'

'What's she want to come here for?' Warrington asked.

'Here, Warrington, this ain't bleedin' *Mastermind*! You got any questions, ask her yourself. I'm just following orders. Just like you are, pal!'

'Listen, Leary, I already said I'm sorry… You know Charlie's always been a bit of a handful, but since he met that Dunstable, he's really changed for the worse. He's making a packet of money. Spends all his time on Dunstable's business now. I don't care for that bloke. Real smarmy beggar. Talks to you like he found you stuck on the sole of his shoe.'

'Yeah, well, there was plenty like him around in the army. All those up-your-backside Ruperts shouting the odds! Never been in a real teeth-kicking scrap in their whole lives, then talking down to you, like they seen it all,' Leary observed, disgust in his voice.

'Charlie really hates your guts, you know,' Warrington said reflectively. 'But you can't tell what's going on in Dunstable's head.'

'Well, cheers for telling me that, Warrington! And there's me with a white frock in the wardrobe, thinking Charlie's about to propose.'

'I'm only being straight with you.' Warrington lowered his voice. 'This Truman woman. She's a funny, posh beggar an' all. I reckon she's a bit "touched" if you ask me.'

He tapped his head significantly.

'Well, you'd know, wouldn't you?' Leary commented.

Warrington shook his head, frustrated again at Leary's talent for getting under his skin.

'Ah, she's harmless enough. Educated sort, really. Mind you—' Leary began.

'Uncle Garry!' Ray called over.

Leary walked across to his nephew. Across the hedge and far into the next pasture beyond they could see a lone figure walking. The red beret and strangely graceful manner in which it moved meant it could only be Zita Truman.

Warrington took the binoculars and focused them on the isolated figure in the field.

'What's she doing? Look, she's practically up to her thighs in mud in that ploughed bit. Keeps sinking down, then pulling each leg out. She's in a right old mess! What's she doing?' he demanded.

'I don't know… Taking a closer look,' Leary guessed.

Miss Truman made a strange sight moving awkwardly across the ploughed mud of the fields. She was dressed completely inappropriately for the terrain, in muddied tweed trousers, lilac jacket, cream blouse and an open mackintosh, which flapped in the wind.

'What's she doing?' Warrington asked again.

'Jeez! How many more times, Warrington?' Leary replied, exasperated.

The minutes passed as Miss Truman negotiated two gates and two more fields. She was now crossing the road and approaching the base's fence about a hundred metres from the main entrance. The surveillance cameras on the perimeter had all swung slowly in her direction.

'Flaming funny reconnaissance,' Warrington observed.

'What the hell's she doing?'

'Look, Warrington!' began Leary, fiercely, 'I've told you what she's doin'... Oh my good Gawd!' Leary exclaimed. 'What's she doin'?'

For Zita Truman had grasped the fence.

TWENTY

Jeremy Brint reset his figures on the laptop, just out of sight of the prisoner, and nodded to Professor Morris to indicate he could continue. Morris checked the wrist straps which had seriously dug into the prisoner's flesh during that last question. He eased them by a notch. The squaddie, sitting behind Brint in the corner, stood up to look intently at what was being done before settling back in his seat and yawning.

The prisoner was slumped in the chair, his head into his chest. Morris checked out all the vital signs and could see nothing from the readings to suggest there was anything of a life-threatening nature to interrupt the work. Blood pressure was a little high, certainly, but the pulse was strong and steady.

He took a moment to read through the questions again and checked out the graphs in relation to the prisoner's responses – or lack of them! He found himself yawning again.

'Corporal Ball,' he called out to the squaddie, 'would you mind fetching me another coffee?'

Brint, the little swine, looked up from the laptop to indicate his need for a stimulant.

'Make that two, Corporal,' Morris ordered reluctantly.

Fetching coffee for two skanky boffins in a detention centre was hardly what Corporal John Ball had enlisted for years ago. He'd visited a detention centre in Iraq once, at the invitation of a Green Beret whose kit he'd borrowed on a couple of occasions. The Yanks were alright about stuff like that. British troops went around regularly cadging Yank equipment. Their kit was top of the range.

The place had been a madhouse, but at least it delivered results! Here it was all tiptoeing round like pansies! Ball couldn't even understand the point of half the questions they asked. On some occasions he and Brint had even been requested to leave the room while toffee-nosed Morris carried on his stupid bloody kids' game.

Mind you, what was the point of him being here anyway? Ball reflected. The prisoner looked as threatening as one of those kittens in a cup you saw on the internet, and he cried like a bleedin' baby!

'Please remember, cream in mine,' Morris added, fed up with how often Ball forgot.

That and my spit, Ball thought, his way of taking revenge on that arrogant, look-down-your-nose prat!

'Of course, sir,' Ball replied, smiling unctuously. 'I'll make sure—'

The blare of the hooter caused Morris to spontaneously clasp his hands to his ears. He had never heard the damned thing before, and its decibel level physically hurt the eardrums. Ball, who had also never heard it before either, stopped at the doorway and looked down the corridor towards the reception area.

The prisoner raised his head suddenly and appeared to look up intently at the furthermost corner of the room, though his eyes were still closed.

'What's happening? What do we do?' Morris shouted over the din.

'Well, you can shut it for a start!' Ball replied, delighted for once to be giving the orders.

TWENTY-ONE

Warrington dropped the binoculars and stepped back. Ray picked them up and looked. Smoke arose from the figure and great arcs of electrical, blue light came from the fence, together with the most appalling cacophony of sirens, hooters and alarm bells. Miss Truman seemed to tear the fence apart like paper, and then burst through the gap, leaving strips of the mackintosh flapping in the wind on both sides.

Leary and Warrington were each backing away, utterly stupefied. The sound of clunking metal, muffled shots and dull explosions could be heard. Crows in the trees around them had wheeled up, startling the three further. The two men roused themselves.

'Jesus! Let's get the hell out of here!' Leary shouted.

'What about Miss Truman?' Ray cried.

'Sod Miss Truman!'

Ray faltered, then followed them. Leary reached the vehicle first, slammed down the open bonnet and jumped in behind the wheel. He searched his pockets desperately for the keys.

'Jesus! Jesus!' he kept repeating. 'Where's the soddin' keys?'

Warrington had taken up the passenger seat, so Ray climbed in the back. He became aware of a very strong smell of diesel.

Leary finally found the keys to the accompaniment of Warrington's cursing him. The engine misfired, stalled and then, finally, came alive. The van shot away, bouncing wildly over the ploughed field; Leary, his foot jammed on the accelerator, barely able to control the steering. It kangarooed as it got nearer the field entrance, misfired, moved again and then stopped.

Dead.

Leary wrenched the ignition key, draining the battery. He swore furiously at the stranded vehicle while the sound of distant clunks of metal and more distinct gunshots continued in the background.

Then... Silence.

Looking back across the fields Ray saw a figure suddenly appear, bursting through a hedge some 300 metres away. He shouted to his uncle who was slumped in his seat and had discovered the van's fault. The fuel gauge showed empty.

'You bloody idiot!' Warrington shouted at him.

Leary shook his head in disbelief. 'There was half a tank of diesel in there. I know there was...'

Ray saw Miss Truman within a hundred metres of them; at least it was her head and beret. The torso was still clothed but the jacket arms and trouser bottoms were tattered, smoking strips. A flap of skin on her forehead whipped back and forth above her right eye socket as she raced towards them, with a long, oval-shaped, silver rucksack-style bag slung over her shoulders.

Ray pushed open the rear doors and she laid the bag gently on the van floor.

She looked him closely in the eyes, strangely detached from the immediate situation, as if all the calamities around her were a figment of some twisted imagination.

'Thank you, Raymond. I am extremely regretful that my actions have placed you in a position of severe peril. I appear to have been motivated to undertake these ridiculously uncontemplated actions by "feelings" I have never experienced before. Please do accept my most sincere apologies,' she said calmly.

Closing the doors, she went around to the driver's side. Leary looked appalled at the flapping skin, and what looked like dull metal underneath.

'What the hell's going on? Who the hell are you?' he shouted in Miss Truman's face.

'We are in severe jeopardy, Mr Leary. Place the gear transmission in neutral.'

'What?! What's the bloody point? The van's kaput! Finished!' shouted Leary.

'Do it now, Mr Leary, or we will all face annihilation.'

Leary could make out the distant sound of a helicopter powering up and personnel carriers moving. Zita Truman disappeared around the back of the van while Leary put the gear in neutral, felt the van suddenly accelerate and tried desperately to steer through the gate.

He need not have bothered. Within seconds the van

had reached sixty, with Miss Truman controlling both the speed and the direction. How she was navigating was a mystery, but she successfully managed to avoid a head-on collision with the only other vehicle they encountered down the country back lanes, ripping out one of the van's side panels as she moved a little too far to the left and caught the edge of a rock sticking out of the embankment.

Looking out of the back window and seeing her middle-aged, beret-covered head with the flap of skin bob up and down in time with her run was surreal. Ray looked at the oval-shaped bag on the van floor, which had what seemed like scorch marks across it.

They moved at breakneck speed with the poor road surfaces bouncing them around and the vehicle's suspension making sickening noises. Warrington sat shocked and terrified, clinging for life to the seat belt he hadn't had time to fasten. Leary was thrown backwards and forwards but clung on fast to the steering wheel, as if he still had some control over his destiny.

On three occasions, Truman had had to dig her heels into the road surface and pull the vehicle to a halt as it overshot particularly acute bends and careered into a dry-stone wall, hedge and field. Ray had found himself tumbling around the van's interior like a lottery ball number, but finally managed to get his hands a purchase of sorts on some wooden storage struts.

He had no idea how long this insane flight lasted, but the van suddenly turned sharply and jolted and leapt like a crazed mustang along a farm track. It stopped suddenly, throwing Ray forwards onto the floor against the oval-shaped bundle, which hadn't moved from its position once during the entire, bone-jarring journey.

The silence, after all the noise before, seemed palpable. Miss Truman collected the bag and carried it into a deserted building. The rest of the van's occupants stumbled out to find themselves in a small clearing in a copse, with an abandoned farmhouse before them, the roof half exposed and what looked like an outhouse attached.

The van was wrecked. Two deep indentations, with finger marks embedded in the metal at the rear, marked where Miss Truman's hands had gripped and steered it. The bodywork was dented, torn, scratched and the back suspension apparently broken, with the wheels resting on the inside of the arches. The front was a mangled mess with bits of stone wall and foliage stuck in it.

They stumbled into the dank darkness after her and sank to the muddy stone floor across the other side of the room to where the silver bag lay, which Miss Truman was tending. Leary fumbled for his tobacco and papers, clumsily rolled a cigarette, lit it and inhaled deeply.

Miss Truman got up and moved outside. They heard the scraping, screeching and tearing of metal, exploding glass, falling masonry and a shuddering in the walls.

Then. Silence.

'Jesus! What's she doing now?' Leary asked, like a weary, played-out dad too tired to care about his children's noises in the next room.

TWENTY-TWO

'What the...' Major General Phillips muttered as his car drove around the bend and up to the entrance of the Derringham base.

The main road had been cordoned off a half a mile back and traffic was being redirected. He had been contacted at home, just fifteen minutes earlier, and the scene which met his eyes appalled him. Just inside the main gates two armoured personnel carriers lay turned over on their backs with another one resting on top of them at a crazy angle, its front wheels twisted. Soldiers in full battledress were scurrying around the scene.

The driver pulled up and Phillips got out and squeezed past the upended vehicles. A breathless captain ran up to him, making a hurried salute.

'Sir... We... That is...' he began.

Phillips recognised the after-effects of shock in the man's eyes and trembling jaw.

'Alright. Alright, Thompson,' he broke in, 'take your time.'

'Sir, I...I have to report that the... the perimeter has been breached... and the base compromised,' Thompson finally got out.

That's some gift for understatement, Phillips thought, looking at the trail of destruction.

'Casualties?'

'About... about fifteen we know of so far, sir. No seriously injured as yet.'

Phillips was pleased to note that Thompson was getting a grip again. He was a first-class officer – intelligent, diligent, reliable and commanding troops considered the finest in the world. It must have been some attack to throw someone of his considerable military experience off-guard.

'Who's responsible for all this?' Phillips asked.

He indicated rows of white vans and civilian cars they were passing, all with holes punched through the bonnets and, in some cases, the engines resting on the tarmac below.

'We... we just don't know, sir.'

Between two of the buildings another military vehicle lay on its side, fuel spreading across the ground. Men in protective gear were beginning to foam it down.

'Building 7's prisoner... He's gone, sir,' Thompson finally admitted, like a cowed schoolboy plucking up the courage to tell a strict teacher he'd forgotten his homework.

Phillips stopped on the spot. 'Gone?!'

'Escaped, sir.'

'All this... for the breakout of one man?' Phillips asked incredulously.

'As far as we can tell, sir.'

They had reached Building 7, an anonymous-looking office block. The front was lying in a twisted mess of aluminium framing and shattered glass. A white-coated man, Morris, ran out to meet them – another victim of shock, Phillips noted.

'He's... he's gone! Another one took him!' he cried wildly.

'What? What's that, Morris?' Phillips demanded.

Phillips was becoming angry. He wanted facts and all he was getting were disjointed ramblings. This looked like the mother of all domestic military disasters and he was already anticipating the inevitable, painful 'Official Inquiry'.

'Sir! Captain Thompson, sir!'

A sergeant ran over. He looked fully in control of his faculties, Phillips noted.

'Beg pardon, sir', the sergeant added, recognising Phillips and addressing the more senior officer. 'No reports of any other intruders on the base. It seems it was just the one, sir.'

'One?!' Phillips asked. 'One man has done all this? Who?' he asked, not expecting a reply.

'Actually, sir... The general description, sir...' the sergeant swallowed, 'is that of a middle-aged woman... in a red hat...'

'*A woman in a red hat?!*'

Phillips thought for a moment and then turned to the trembling figure in the white coat beside him.

'Tell me, Professor Morris,' he demanded viciously, 'just who or what the hell have we been guarding here for the past five months?'

TWENTY-THREE

Zita Truman reappeared and went over to the oval bundle. She had her back to Ray who couldn't see what she was doing. There was a barely audible sound of electrical fizzing coming from her and Ray saw that her left hand was jerking spasmodically.

Ray's mouth felt ridiculously dry; he could barely move his tongue around it. He had a bottle of water, but it had been bounced out of his pocket during the crazy journey. He stood up shakily and went to retrieve it.

'Where do you think you're off?' Leary asked him wearily.

'I left some water in the van.'

'No, you don't, boy. Too dangerous.'

Leary hauled himself upright and stumbled outside.

He saw that the van had been pushed into the outhouse. Its passage had brought down the lintel and surrounding brickwork and had torn and concertinaed part of the metal roof. He managed to get one of the rear doors open enough to squeeze his arm inside and grasp the bottle.

Stepping back, Leary saw method in Truman's madness; the van wouldn't be spotted from the air at least.

Back in the building he saw a figure lying against the opposite wall, the metal shroud covering him from the neck down. He was momentarily shocked by how ill and frail he looked. His complexion was grey, his eyes wild and hunted, and there were the imprints of small circles across his skull and face, where electrodes had been attached.

Leary and Ray were in a state of shock, but Warrington seemed particularly crushed and traumatised. He was sitting slumped, staring emptily at the ground. Leary passed the bottle to Ray who drank and then shared it between himself and Warrington.

A real good kid, Leary thought, looking at Ray, sitting with his eyes fixed on the glassless window opposite. *Decent. Not one word of complaint or whining about what has been happening throughout this whole sorry, bloody mess.* And how had Leary repaid him for all that trust and patience? Dropped him slap bang down in the middle of a piggin' catastrophe! Put his life in danger!

He hadn't meant to! 'Course he hadn't bloody meant to! But he'd somehow managed it all the same! Story of his life really – causing mayhem through not being arsed enough about things! At that moment there wasn't one scumbag he had more contempt for than Garry Stinking Leary! He'd get the lad out of this, no matter what shenanigans it took. He still had a couple of aces up his sleeve.

He looked across at the Truman woman, thing, whatever it was and felt cold fury and an opportunity to vent some of the scorn he felt for himself towards her/it, as well! He'd bloody well sort her out one way or another!

The figure in the shroud began to focus on Leary, Warrington and Ray, and a look of naked panic and terror came over his face. He pushed himself back hard against the wall. Leary broke the silence.

'That him, is it, Zita? That your long-lost bro? The one I got screwed over for? The one they're going to blow us all to beggary about? 'Cos, I got to tell you, Zita love, he's no catwalk model, is he? We're looking at lifetime sentences here if we're lucky. And the boy…'

He paused, surprised to find himself suddenly choked up.

'You are entitled to an explanation,' Miss Truman said quietly, 'and I very much regret what has occurred, particularly with regard to Raymond.'

She stood up, facing them.

'I would ask you first to believe me when I say that it was not my intention to infiltrate that facility, but as I approached it, my companion's pain, distress and closeness to non-existence became all too apparent to me. I could only sense it to the exclusion of all else.

'As you may have deduced, we are not of this world. Our mission was to explore this planet, learn from it and gain the insight we need to metamorphose into our next stage of development. Only a very few of our species undertake this hazardous procedure.

'There are precedents for such behaviours in your own human species. A "rite of passage" you term it; an experience that marks the transition from one state of development to another. In Australia the Aboriginal goes on "Walkabout". In the Sikh ceremony of Amrit Sanchar both girls and boys are initiated into the Khalsa. In—'

'In ten minutes, we'll all be dead, love!' Leary shouted. 'Now, that's a real interesting "transition from one state of development to another", Zita, but none of us here fancies it much. Do you see? Are you getting it?'

'Mr Leary, I am trying to explain why we are in our current situation.'

'No, you ain't. You're giving us your faffin' version of Wikipedia and we ain't got the time, see. We got other things on our mind, like how the hell we don't end up splattered all over the walls of this place when some helicopter gunship homes in on us! Are you getting it now?!'

'Mr Leary, you are expressing yourself in a brutal manner again. This is unnecessarily distressing.'

'Distressing? I'll tell you what's distressing, Zita! Getting a twenty-millimetre, high-velocity cannon shell in your ear hole! That's distressing! That don't half scramble your brain and bring the tears to your eyes. They're going to have troops combing all round here. Do you get it? So, what's the plan, Zita? What's the plan?'

'A solution?' she asked.

'What?' Leary asked, exasperated.

'You are looking for a solution to our problem. You do not wish to explore the nature of the problem?' she asked.

'What you talkin' about?' Leary demanded, a look of frustration threatening to turn into an explosion of rage.

'You wish only to know how we are to deal with the present situation in such a way as to extricate ourselves from it?' she asked.

'Halle-bloody-lujah!' Leary cried. 'Give that… thing a kewpie doll!'

'I do not understand that last reference, Mr Leary. However, I do have a strategy for escape,' she said.

'Oh well, that's nice. Maybe you could share it with us. You know, before we all finish up in bits, like.'

Warrington seemed finally to have roused himself from the deep stupor he'd settled into. He staggered to his feet.

'How many has she killed?' he cried to Leary, pointing at Truman. 'How many?! I'm not going to prison for murder and terrorism!'

He made for the door-opening as Zita Truman took up a position directly in front of it. Warrington made to shove her out of the way. It was like watching an infant pushing at a tank. She didn't budge. He stepped back, dropped his shoulder, and launched himself at her, as he would against a locked door, before ricocheting back. Miss Truman remained rigid and immoveable. Warrington, in gasping, shameful exasperation, drew back his fist and smashed it as hard as possible at the side of her head. It made a dull, metallic, clunk sound.

Zita Truman didn't blink, flinch or move, but a howl of outraged pain came from Warrington.

'Jeeeez!' he screamed out, holding the damaged hand.

'She's some kind of mechanism, Warrington,' Leary observed wearily. 'What good do you think thumping her's likely to do?'

'Mr Warrington,' Zita Truman explained patiently, 'my companion and I find ourselves in extremely desperate circumstances. We have very specific guidelines for missions which absolutely forbid harm to other species we encounter. However, on such a lethal planet as this, I am afraid I have been having serious doubts as to whether we can follow them.'

'What?' Warrington asked, his pained expression turning to puzzlement.

'To put it in idiot terms you can understand, Jonas, I think she's just threatened to punch your head in, pal. So, I'd sit down again if I was you,' Leary helpfully translated.

Warrington, nursing his hand between his upper arm and body, looked at her a moment and then returned to sit, his shoulders hunched, in the furthest corner of the room from her.

The sound of a helicopter came from somewhere in the distance.

'I need to take my companion to safety,' Miss Truman continued and then turned to Ray. 'Raymond, I must ask for your help and kindness in assisting my companion—'

'Listen, Zita,' Leary interrupted angrily, 'he's not going anywhere, right? And we're not moving till we've had some questions answered. Do you get that? Now, what exactly happened at that base?'

'My companion was being held there against his will. The humans there were "researching" him.'

She looked to the Companion to continue the account. The Companion spoke, his voice halting and weak.

'Please… excuse my sense of… profound disgust. I am finding it very difficult to be in such… such close proximity to you. You are, without doubt, the most vindictive and vicious species we have ever encountered.'

'Oh, cheers, pal. That's real nice of you, but do you think we could—' Leary began.

'It was terrible. Terrible! That one living creature could subject another to such humiliation; pain.'

'Was the pain very severe?' Zita Truman asked the Companion.

He shook his head. 'No. No, you do not understand. The physical pain was tolerable; savage clumsiness. What was unbearable was the callousness of the minds of those who worked on me. They seemed only to possess one belief: an absurd compulsion to reduce all things, including my suffering, into banal pieces of data.

'They actually prided themselves on their intellectual superiority and their ability to detach themselves from feeling. Absolutely abhorrent! I simply cannot comprehend how beings capable of feeling, possessing an intelligence which can produce self-consciousness and imagination, could possibly subject another living creature to such barbarity... We should not have come here.'

Leary, furious, interrupted. 'You're really not getting this, are you, chummy? To be brutally honest, I ain't really interested in what they done to you. Yeah? What I want to know is what the hell happened back there? How many people did she kill or maim?'

'I have killed no one, Mr Leary,' Zita Truman interrupted. 'I damaged buildings and immobilised vehicles I encountered, but I did no significant injury to anyone. Those people, on the other hand, have subjected my companion to months of torture and degradation for no apparent reason.'

'Oh well, that's alright then, isn't it?' said Leary breezily. 'Tell you what, why don't we all pop home for tea and ginger beer in what's left of the van, and send 'em a five-shilling postal order for the damage?

'Jesus, Zita!' Leary, outraged, continued. 'You've just taken on the British Army, destroyed a military base and landed us in a hovel in the middle of nowhere, with no frickin' transport!'

'I regret this,' she said simply.

'"I regret this"! Is that it? That the best you got to offer? 'Cos I'm telling you, you lame-brained, ugly—'

'Uncle Garry,' Ray began, getting up from the floor, 'this isn't right.'

He was feeling ashamed again of the brutal manner in which his uncle was behaving.

'Listen, boy, don't you even start!' Leary shouted. 'These maniacs from some other muckin' planet have come here on some kind of awayday, piggin' holiday. Right? They'll beggar off when they're done. We got to live here!

'So, don't you look down your nose and get all smart and superior with me again, sunshine, 'cos you ain't done the time or earned the right, see? I want to know what she's going to do to get us out of the crap she's just landed us in! Do you understand? So, as far as you're concerned, boy, you just sit yourself back down there and keep it shut! Right?!'

Ray looked down, squeezed his eyes shut and then looked up again. He saw the things that were Miss Truman and her companion looking vulnerable, broken, kindly and dignified, and his uncle bullying, full of self-righteous rage.

And, in his mind, he saw the taunting Leon Rogers at school and his laughing nastiness; and Manley with his thuggish stupidity; and Dunstable with his superior cruelty; and Dad with his dismissive disappointment in him; and Mum with her conditional love – conditional if he did things her way. And he shouted, almost screeched as loud as he could at his uncle.

'It's Raymond, you bloody bastard! It's Raymond! It's not "boy" or "son"! It's bloody Raymond! And why can't you treat people right?!'

He stood there, tears starting from his eyes, his shoulders shaking, and a curious sense of tingling released in his body, as if some massive dam had finally burst inside him.

Leary, startled and shocked, looked as if he'd just been slapped. He'd been telling the kid to toughen up, but he'd certainly not expected something like this off him!

'Once again, Raymond,' Miss Truman began after a long pause, 'I am indebted to you for your decency, honesty, empathy, kindness and consideration. Why are these such rare, rare qualities in this world?

'You are right in part, Mr Leary,' she continued, 'though you express yourself again in the most aggressive and repugnant manner possible. My plan is to draw away the pursuers while you return my companion to the town of Brookdale-on-Sea. There he will rendezvous with the Other.'

'What? Hang on! The "Other"? What "Other"?' Leary demanded.

'There are three of us, Mr Leary,' Miss Truman said simply.

TWENTY-FOUR

Phillip Faulkner, Director for Homeland Security, had just swallowed down two more paracetamols for what seemed like his permanent headache. A large Scotch had assisted their passage down his gullet. The day had been passing painlessly enough right up until Stephen Greenhawn, that idiot Head of Cybernet Intelligence, had come blundering in.

'Sir, the internet's going crazy! There's been some kind of incident at Derringham Commando Training Base. It's in Devon.'

How the hell did a slimy toad like Greenhawn find out this kind of information well before the head of the organisation did, Faulkner wondered again. Bloody world wide web, of course!

'Thank you, Greenhawn. I know where the damned base is located. What kind of incident?'

'Well, it sounds like some kind of attack on it!'

Faulkner's heart actually missed a beat. Greenhawn passed across a tablet displaying photos, texts and emails they had intercepted.

Oh, God! The most appalling of all Faulkner's appalling nightmares was becoming reality!

'Who's sending this stuff out?' he demanded.

'Civilians on the base and motorists.'

'Lock it down! I want all servers to that base and surrounding areas within a fifty-mile radius shutting down immediately. Do you understand?'

'I can't do that without written authorisation!' Greenhawn challenged.

Faulkner grabbed a notepad and wrote rapidly in block capitals: '*SHUT DOWN THE SERVERS AT DERRINGHAM IMMEDIATELY, YOU ARSE!*'

'How's that?' he asked, showing Greenhawn.

'Sir, that's an official memo!'

'You're right. Let's scrub "arse". That'll be our little secret. Now do it! And, before you go, is Windridge still on the premises?'

'Pardon?'

'Is. Windridge. Still. Here?' Faulkner enunciated, as if he were talking to a total idiot.

'Er... I think so... Sir, I've been meaning to speak to you again about Windridge. Attitude and general aptitude are well below par, sir.'

'You really want to speak to me about personnel issues at a moment like this, Greenhawn? Really?'

'My department's suffering. General Assurance rated me at only three on the last performance indicator. It's affecting my output, sir!'

'I don't give a damn how it's affecting your bloody bowel movements! I want them! Now! You understand? And get hold of Spencer too. Now, Greenhawn!'

The news from Derringham had pole-axed Faulkner. That pathetic-looking figure being held at the barracks was, apparently, an 'alien'. Not an 'alien' illegal immigrant; that would have been easy to sort. Not a terrorist; even easier. Not a Soviet spy; an absolute doddle to handle.

No, what they had there down at Derringham was, seemingly, a genuine creature from a planet outside the solar system. If Morris had done his job properly, precautions could, perhaps, have been taken to increase security by moving it to some other location. But, dammit, Derringham was as secure as it got anywhere! Now there were at least two of the bloody things apparently!

What did this all add up to? An invasion?!

Faulkner knew that other foreign intelligence service chiefs would soon be on his back, for he had informed none of the NATO allies. The Yanks, for one, would be furious.

So why had he not informed them? Because until this moment he'd never really believed it. He'd observed this 'alien' through the two-way mirror at Morris's research facility – a mute, sick-looking, middle-aged man, as frightening and threatening as a traumatised bunny rabbit! The only unusual things about him were the device he'd had with him and how absolutely, ridiculously normal and mundane he'd looked!

Homeland Security Operations were always picking up sad types who fancied they could change the world with an impassioned 'Tweet' or the threat of a terrorist outrage. Most had subsequently to be referred on to the secure wings of mental hospitals. For there were two things he could absolutely rely on in his line of work: a seemingly unlimited supply of 'headcases', and wholly inadequate resources with which to investigate them. Neither the Government nor even the Prime Minister had been notified. Informing them was going to be interesting!

Pride, that was another thing that had tripped Faulkner up. Standing before his peers and stating that he suspected that he might have a little middle-aged man from outer space in his custody would have been a grand way of announcing his unfitness for any government office.

So, he'd underplayed it. As a result, he would have to face those peers, admit his 'incompetence' and probably resign before they pushed him. Since his record up to this point had been pretty well exemplary, perhaps they might not terminate his employment quite so swiftly.

Only himself, James Marchbank, a friend, and Director of Foreign Affairs Operations, Professor Morris, and the informer, codenamed 'Cheryl', had any knowledge of the thing. Marchbank, a man whose judgement was first rate, had totally agreed with the low-key approach. Faulkner would keep his name out of it when the inevitable inquiry began.

The original alien had been apprehended in the County of Devon at some seaside resort, but there was no evidence that it had any connections to it. Indeed, one of its mysteries was the absence of any of the normal government proof of existence all other British and foreign nationals were expected to have.

He knew he should contact Major General Phillips immediately and get an on-the-ground report. But he just couldn't face doing it yet. He would likely live to regret that procrastination as well, he speculated, refilling his glass.

TWENTY-FIVE

'Three? I mean… What? Who?'

Leary struggled to comprehend a sense of betrayal he felt.

'You said there was only one!' he finally managed, outraged.

'I did not, Mr Leary. I hired yourself and Mr Warrington to each find a Mr Truman.'

'You lied!' Leary shouted.

'Impossible. I withheld some facts, but I did not lie. I am not capable of it.'

'You bloody lied!' Leary shouted. 'And I been straight down the line with you.'

A thought suddenly struck Leary. 'What happened to that van when we was at the base?' he asked suspiciously.

'I disconnected the fuel lead,' Miss Truman replied simply.

'You… you disconnected the fuel lead? You bloody maniac! You could've got us all killed!'

'I had calculated that you would abandon me there,' Miss Truman said calmly. 'That was the correct assumption, was it not?'

Leary went to say something, but then thought better of it.

The Companion spoke in tired, faltering tones. 'We must hurry. Every moment we remain here exposes the Other to further corruption. Did you know that he... he has changed his name and identity?'

'Unprecedented,' Miss Truman said.

'I had contacted and was about to confront him. I believe he arranged my removal,' the Companion stated.

'That is the conclusion at which I had arrived, but—' she began.

'Whoa! Whoa! Hang on a piggin' minute! Let me get this straight. One of your own kind shopped you to the authorities?' Leary interrupted.

'Shopped?' the Companion queried.

'Yeah, shopped! Grassed up! Turned over! Betrayed!' Leary fumbled for the right words.

'Yes,' he said.

'Well, jeez, pal! So much for the superior, piggin' species, eh!' Leary snorted.

Zita Truman moved over to the Companion, and they began to speak quietly together. Ray observed the Companion shaking his head, apparently in disagreement, but finally, Miss Truman turned towards them.

'We wish to leave as soon as possible. You will take my companion with you to the town of Brookdale and rendezvous at the headquarters of Vader International at 21.30 hours. I shall draw away any pursuers...'

There was a pause.

'Please,' she added.

'Forget it!' Warrington said, rising unsteadily to his feet.

Miss Truman, reaching under her clothing to the underside of her lower rib cage, withdrew a handful of diamonds and held them out for inspection.

'I do not mean to insult you, but material gain appears to be a high motivator for your species.'

'You can stuff your bloody diamonds!' shouted Warrington. 'I've been strong-armed into all this. I'm not doing it! That's a fact!'

'You got any other brilliant ideas then, Warrington? 'Cos now's the time to share 'em, pal!' Leary challenged.

'I'm not doing it, Leary! We… we go back to the base and hand ourselves in.'

'Oh, what a brilliant piece of strategic bloody thinking that is, Jonas! So, what do you think they're going to do to us then? Give us a big sloppy kiss, brush and shovel, and tell us to clear up the mess!

'It may have escaped your attention, pal, but she's just attacked and wrecked one of the most secure army bases in the country!' Leary continued. 'And we've just transported her there so she could do it! You even helped her out the bloody van, Warrington! We'd have beards down to our bollocks by the time we got out of clink!'

Warrington looked pained and confused.

'Listen', Leary continued, 'this… this thing's just given us a way out and she's offering big money with it, see? And I'm not having some spineless, whingeing twerp mucking it up for me. I'm looking at two to five years straight in the nick minimum for pushing drugs anyway, thanks to your manky mates. If I go in poor, I'm coming out rich.'

'Listen—' Warrington began.

'No, you listen, feller! 'Cos it was your poxy brother-in-law what stitched me up. Right? Now, as it stands, no one knows you're in on this, do they? No one but us four. But you scarper down there and tell all, and I'm going to give you such grief, Warrington, you'll think I pulled your piggin' teeth out via your backside.'

Leary enunciated the points carefully, tapping each finger on his left hand with his right forefinger. 'One: you're an ex-marine grunt, ain't you? So, guess who gave Miss Psycho here all the inside gen on the layout of Derringham? Not me, pal! Never been near the place in me life!

'You what—' Warrington began.

'Two: you been conspiring to keep her whereabouts a secret for the past week.'

'I never—'

'Three: you were here when the breakout took place and shared the piggin' van with her! Four: your car's in the pub car park. If there's cameras round it'll show you happily toddling on board Zita's Death-Ship Muckin' Enterprise! And five: at over six foot tall, how in the hell are me and the boy here supposed to strong-arm you?'

'What are you talking about, Leary?!' Warrington demanded, his eyes bright with indignant fury. 'I didn't organise any breakout and I never knew what she was up to!'

'Well, guess what, Warrington, me old cock? I'll say you did. And she'll say you did, and him, and so will he.'

Leary pointed in turn at Miss Truman, the Companion and Ray.

'Now as it is, Jonas,' continued Leary, 'no one can pin a thing on you except us four, can they? So, here's the choice, pal, nice and simple. You can wise up, play out the hand, get rich and get away from Manley. Or you can do "the right thing" and find yourself dropping down the biggest bog hole, leading to the deepest pile of doo-doo.'

He paused before continuing, 'So, feller, what's it going be?'

Warrington began to say something, closed his mouth, lowered his eyes and sat down again.

'Oh, how jolly, jolly good!' Leary said and turned to Miss Truman. 'Right, you, what's the plan?'

'I shall remove the vehicle from its current location and use it to draw away pursuers, whilst you make your way to the rendezvous point. I shall go now,' she said, making for the door.

Leary and Ray, following her, stood back as she pulled the van out and punched the rest of the smashed windscreen from its frame. Gripping and stretching the corrugated metal roof back, as if it were made of canvas, she secured it by twisting the corners around the van's now bent front pillars.

'Oh, beautiful job, Zita,' Leary remarked ironically, 'but it ain't going to make it on *Wheeler Dealers*, is it?' he added, shaking his head at Truman's handiwork.

'I do not understand that reference either, Mr Leary. Is there anything further to be done?' Miss Truman asked.

'Yeah. Well, don't count on getting your deposit back for a start. Just take the licence plates off, stick 'em inside and get rid of it. Our prints are all over it, see? You could've burned the damned thing, but since you seemed to have drained off the diesel, that's a non-starter.'

'"Non-starter and damned thing with no diesel",' Miss Truman repeated. 'That is one of your attempts at a witticism, Mr Leary?' she asked.

'No, it ain't!' Leary said irritably. 'Just get rid of the sod!'

'I shall destroy it completely. You will have no reason to fear it will be traced back to you,' Miss Truman said.

'Well, thank you so much, Zita. That suddenly makes the whole world look a lot cheerier,' Leary replied insincerely.

She turned from him and went back into the farmhouse. A few moments later she re-emerged and walked across to Ray. She focused her curiously intent but strangely dead eyes on him.

'Raymond, you will please take care of my companion and see that he arrives at the rendezvous. It is vitally important.'

'Yeah, we'll do that,' Leary said.

Miss Truman continued to look at Ray as if she hadn't heard Leary speak.

'Raymond?' she prompted.

'I'll… I'll do me best,' Ray replied awkwardly, though he hadn't a clue how.

'Wait an hour or more,' said Miss Truman, 'to be certain to avoid any pursuers.'

'Yeah. Yeah. I'll do that,' said Leary, peeved he was being by-passed in the conversation in favour of his nephew.

'Thank you, Raymond. I shall never forget the kindnesses you have shown us here,' she said, before turning and setting off to push the van up the track.

There was something ridiculous and pathetic about her departure – the loping gait of a middle-aged woman pushing this travesty of a van up an incline. Ray watched her go and felt unexpectedly emotional. A moment's contemplation explained his feelings.

He had just understood that Zita Truman did not expect to see any of them again.

TWENTY-SIX

'So, Morris, I will ask you once again, what exactly was it that you were doing your research on? A direct, straight answer is all I require!' Phillips demanded.

Morris was sitting slumped in his office chair, Brint twitching nervously next to him and Major General Phillips standing opposite, leaning towards them, his hands on the desk edge. Corporal Ball was being treated in the base infirmary.

Forty-seven minutes had elapsed since the alarms had sounded.

'Well, you can shut it for a start!' Ball had spat out at Morris on first hearing them.

Seconds after the alarm, Morris, Brint and Ball had heard the sound of rifle cracks coming from the area of the base's entrance, some 500 metres away. Morris had followed the corporal down the corridor towards the reception area, continually asking him what was happening.

'Shut it!' Ball had finally exclaimed, stopping

momentarily to put his aggressive face close to Morris's pale one to emphasise the point.

On the way, Ball had collected his SA80 rifle from the weapons rack. His pistol already had a round in the chamber. As they entered the deserted reception area, they could hear the lockdown systems coming into play, as the bolts slid into place across the main doors. The doors and frames were reinforced aluminium and the glass, bulletproof.

Although Ball's walkie-talkie was strangely malfunctioning, he was still expecting the alarms to be silenced at any moment and announcements that the drill was complete and that personnel should await the debriefing. It seemed an odd time to run an exercise, given that all the scientific staff, bar Morris and Brint, were enjoying the weekend off-site. The corporal reasoned that these 'precious, poncey' types were probably considered of little value in a drill, testing the establishment's readiness to respond to attack.

The gunshots and regular, increasingly heavy sounds of clunking metal were disorientating for Ball. Unlike this one, every emergency exercise he'd ever been involved in throughout his military career had never come as a surprise. On any military base, the 'scuttlebutt' – soldiers' gossip – never failed to deliver forewarning. Of course, everyone pretended they had been 'surprised' because that increased their superiors' ratings for their response under 'extremely adverse conditions'.

As Ball and Morris entered the reception area, they saw soldiers hurtling out of the adjacent dormitory building, adjusting their dress, body armour and weaponry and running, their boots clomping loudly on the tarmac, towards the base entrance. There was real urgency to their movements and both men were becoming aware that something extraordinary was occurring.

'Brint!' Morris hollered down the corridor at his colleague. 'Stay with 501!'

As Morris and Ball stood at the doors, looking out of the windows, a few seconds of unnerving nothingness was happening, apart from the slight vibrations in the floor, which coincided with each distant 'clunk' sound.

Ball would feel a complete 'loser' if it turned out that a realistic exercise to assess the base's response to an emergency was simply that, and that he had quietly lost self-control and panicked. His mind, therefore, still refused to entertain the possibility that this was anything other than a drill.

Suddenly, the figure of a marine crashed up against the windows, his back impacting and shaking the glass and window frame before slumping to the ground. Both men instinctively recoiled. Ball looked across at Morris then, just as instinctively, realised that Morris would have absolutely 'zilch' to contribute to his assessment of the situation.

A middle-aged woman in a red beret was approaching the doors. She looked remarkably calm and normal, apart from her clothing which was torn and smoking.

'Please, open the doors, please,' she requested pleasantly.

Ball flicked the safety catch off the rifle and pointed it at her.

'Get away from here! Now!' he shouted.

'Can't… can't we let her in?' Morris asked, eager to grant her sanctuary from whatever had hurled the marine against the glass.

'It's a lockdown, dickhead!' Ball shouted, gesturing with his rifle for the woman to move off. 'That means no one gets in or out!'

'We… we can't let her in?!' Morris asked, incredulous at the callousness being shown.

As Ball took his eyes off the woman to address Morris more forcibly, two mighty crashes sounded simultaneously and the corporal saw that she had punched both her fists clear through the toughened glass on either side of the central locks, keeping the entrance doors closed.

He and Morris backed up to the reception desk.

The woman pushed her arms through, then hugged them together around the edges of the two joined doors and moved steadily forwards. The entire metal frame for that section of the doors and windows tore away from the floor and concrete ceiling above with a metallic tearing and screeching. Glass in the upper sections exploded into showers of fragments. One piece of torn framing sprang back and caught the woman's forehead a glancing blow, but she continued to move steadily forward.

As she cast the doors and frame to the ground and began to trample over them, Ball opened fire with a full three-second burst directly at her stomach. She continued to advance, raising her right hand, the palm facing Ball. Morris saw something like a taser wire fly out and retract as quickly. It hit Ball in the face, and he dropped like a stone, no sound of protest or pain escaping him.

The woman stood a full ten seconds, her face blank but her head rotating from right to left, a fraction of a movement at a time. Then she moved down the corridor. Morris looked on, unable to move. Events were proceeding at a nightmarishly slow rate before his shocked gaze. Nothing that was entering his brain was computing with any experience he'd had before.

Brint, in the interrogation room, watched, detached, as a middle-aged woman in a red hat pushed open the door, approached the unconscious figure of Prisoner 501 in the chair and tore off the straps holding him. She reached under her clothing and drew out what looked like a silver-grey, coiled sleeping bag which she proceeded to pull over the inert body. The opening sealed itself and the woman placed her arms through two straps and carried the covered body like a haversack, back towards the reception area.

Three marines had come charging through the wreckage, ordering Morris to hit the floor. They were young, tough-looking, and terrified.

'Target ahead!' one of them screamed, looking down the corridor, and all three dropped to one knee, tucked their rifles well into their shoulders and fired in unison.

The roar of the firearms was absolutely deafening in the confined space, and Morris's arms and hands clasped ever more tightly around his head, his eyes squeezed shut. He was lying face down amongst glass shards. And, to his astonishment, he became aware that he was sobbing uncontrollably and making sounds of pure, animal terror.

'Please, please, God, let me only be safe, a thousand miles away from here and I'll never do another wrong thing again in my life!' he found himself praying to a deity he normally considered a pathetic mental fabrication.

The firing stopped in quick stages as each marine collapsed and Morris, curiosity overcoming his terror, tentatively opened his eyes to see the woman's legs pass by, not a metre from him. He felt bullets slam into the wall above as four other soldiers opened fire from outside the building, each collapsing quickly one after another.

He had no idea how long he lay there, but gradually became aware that the sounds of shots and that heavy clunking sound were distant and receding. He forced his eyes open and his limbs to move, as he crawled over to Ball's body.

The corporal looked as if he were sleeping peacefully. There was a slight red mark on his cheek, but Morris detected a pulse from the neck that was steady, strong and nowhere near the frenzied rate his own was.

He and Ball had somehow survived! For the first time in his existence, he knew that sense of animal euphoria that comes from simply being alive!

TWENTY-SEVEN

Ten minutes after Truman's departure from the farmhouse, a helicopter could be heard heading inland in the opposite direction to Brookdale-on-Sea. Leary and Warrington set off to find transport while Ray stayed behind with the Companion. He helped him out of the shroud and the Companion practised walking, with Ray providing support. His muscles had wasted, and Ray could see how very sick he was.

As they walked outside, the Companion said little to begin with, but Ray found it hard not to feel drawn towards him. There was the same basic honesty of Miss Truman, but it was considerably softened by a gentleness and kindness, clearly overwhelmed by the brutal treatment it had received at the base.

Outside, the Companion stopped to watch the progress of another helicopter overhead. From the conversation which developed, Ray gleaned a good insight into his experiences. His areas of research were the planet's culture and 'spirituality', as he termed it. He had taken accommodation at the flat Leary and Ray had been to visit, which he used as a refuge from which to visit libraries, universities, colleges, religious places of worship, sports arenas, charities, museums, galleries, cinemas and theatres.

He had never ventured further than Exeter and Ray wondered why this particular area had been selected for what appeared to be a major intergalactic research mission. London, some 200 miles away, would surely have provided more cultural opportunities. He said as much, but the Companion shook his head.

'Where we land is really quite arbitrary and research only a secondary part of our mission. The primary purpose of our time here is a test of ourselves to prepare for future growth. The enforced isolation of each of us from the other is an essential part of that process. We must attempt to integrate with the most advanced forms of species on a planet in order to understand and identify with them. Having identified with them, we must come to terms with their impact on us and grow to embrace it.' He paused. 'Does this make sense to you?'

'I think so. I'm not that smart, but I can follow most of what you're saying.'

'You see,' the Companion continued, his passion overcoming his fatigue, 'the predominance of your one species of Homo Sapiens has posed many, many problems for us. Never in all our records of exploration has one single species so totally dominated a world, and this is massively complicated by the apparently diverse behaviours within the species itself.'

'How do you mean?' Ray asked.

'Although you are one species there is an incredibly wide and often contrasting range of attitudes, manners and cultural activities within it. Religions, for example, continue to be a major influence in how you govern your planet's affairs. Faiths are usually a primitive species' attempt to understand their role in a wider cosmos. They are intended to make the believer conscious of their inferiority to a greater, wiser, more magnanimous power in the universe. They should be levelling exercises.'

'"Levelling exercises"?' Ray asked.

'Yes, they should make all creatures feel at the same level; equally humble. After all, if one believes in the concept of an all-powerful entity ruling the entire cosmos, how could that be anything other than a humbling experience? To place any value at all on one's own significance or self-importance as a living creature, in comparison with that gargantuan concept, is, surely, insanely egotistical'.

'Sorry,' Ray said, 'I've lost you.'

'Well, here, for example, even within one faith such as Christianity, there are groups which appear to mistrust and vilify each other for reasons purely of competitive power and control. The Protestant fights the Catholic; the Baptist denies the Mormon.

'When we look across the range of faith communities, these divisions appear even more extreme and absurd. The Muslim faith preaches love, as does the Christian, but still they fight, torture and kill each other. We knew a little of these divisions from our pre-mission preparation but could not have begun to appreciate how fragmented and violently opposed to each other you are capable of being. It is impossible for me to comprehend how faith in an omnipotent, loving deity translates into hatred, mayhem, murder and warfare.'

Despite his low opinion of his intellectual abilities, Ray was intelligent, reflective and honest. What the Companion had just said seemed to suddenly result in a sizeable crack through many of his preconceptions! His faith in Catholicism had been sagging for some months; the Companion's observations seemed to tilt it at a very unstable angle. He felt uncomfortable and exposed.

'Fighting and warfare,' the Companion continued, 'your inefficient and destructive means of resolving problems between groups or nations by the use of indiscriminate violence, appear to be constant factors in your recorded history. After each world conflict you commit yourselves never to repeat such foolish, vicious slaughter, and then embark on it again as soon as your collective memories of the trauma start to fade.

'Even days of remembrance for the deceased can resemble pride in a country's historical, military might over other nations. Indeed, the clarion call to fight, whether it be against other nations, ideologies or even diseases such as cancer, seems to be one of the few motivations for action that unite you. I can appreciate that as a species you have had to fight your way out of the primeval swamp to survive and propagate, but those times are surely past. Why do you simply not accept your vulnerability to violence and disease, mourn the dead on all sides, both military and civilian in the case of conflict, and resolve to help each other?'

Ray looked bewildered. 'I… I don't know.'

'Even in times of peace and within one relatively small area as we have explored here, there are tensions and conflicts between different-coloured skin pigmentations; female and male; old and young; the poor and the wealthy; believers in political systems and those with contrary views. As I observed, you seem to need an "enemy" to focus your energies upon. You appear to have little appreciation that you all share the same, basic traits and characteristics of a species.

'These tensions appear to be present within the family unit, and even within the individual itself. A species so at war with itself has never been identified before. And what is most extraordinary is that so few of you appear to be even aware of these challenges and tensions.'

'Well… Why is that?' Ray asked.

'It is very, very difficult to comprehend, since each and every one of you carries, within your skull, the most sophisticated, dynamic, organic material in the known universe. You have brains of immense complexity and potential power, of which your consciousness is merely the tip. And yet you appear to distract your minds with entertainments and trivia.

'You seem to recognise that your populations are growing, your resources diminishing, your planet struggling to support your demands and needs and yet you never begin to embrace an understanding of the disaster facing you. You are like dwellers in a burning home, who see the flames and smoke all around them and yet continue to throw the most flammable materials upon the conflagration.

'This is both bizarre and profoundly unnatural. In every other civilisation we know of in the universe, existing generations' first concern is that their progeny be in the most advantageous conditions possible to guarantee future, flourishing growth.

'Here, humans appear to sacrifice their offspring's futures for the attainment of their own immediate comfort and desires. This is utterly at odds with every notion we have previously had of species' drive for survival.'

Although Ray was only partially following the Companion's observations, he found it reassuring that the highly intelligent figure before him shared his confusion in the face of human beings' challenges and responses to them.

'So, why can't we deal with things better?' he asked.

'Raymond,' the Companion observed, 'I have to inform you that, even from this brief acquaintance, I have recognised that you are not, at all, typical of the species. You listen, an activity I have found very rare here. You seem devoid of egotism, another rarity. And you, apparently, want to learn something from discourses with others. Practically unheard of in my experience of the adult population of this world.

'Those rare traits are crucial in recognising and addressing crises. And, perhaps, there is another clue to your drift towards self-destruction through wilful ignorance. Non-existence, or "death" as you term it with such dread, appears to be something of a deciding factor. Death awaits all organic creatures and yet your species struggles with this. Indeed, you seem to do all that you can to ignore or disguise that simple, inevitable, biological and universal fact.

'From this one could deduce that terror of death dominates much of your conscious and unconscious thought processes. Perhaps you are simply too terrified to look at reality. Given how traumatic my own time here has been, that is comparatively easy to understand.'

The Companion stopped and, bending painfully, scooped up a handful of shale and pebbles from the farm track. He poured them from one hand to the other, breathed in the earthy smell and, smiling, let them fall.

'Yes. We appear to have set ourselves a seemingly impossible task,' he concluded, 'to reconcile a myriad of contradictions within one consciousness. To put it more simply: to understand what it means to be "human".'

Ray asked what areas Miss Truman and the Other had been responsible for.

'The one you call Miss Truman has a dual role. She has overall responsibility for the mission, but also collects data on your intellectual and scientific achievements, which are extremely impressive for a species of such relatively early development.

'Our other companion,' he continued, 'has had the most perilous task. He was to undertake primary research into your physical and emotional make-up. I fear for him.'

'But he betrayed you, didn't he?' Ray pointed out.

'That is a simplistic interpretation,' the Companion answered. 'He could have no idea of the risks he took when he committed himself to experiencing the sensations of being alive, as you creatures on Earth do. Perhaps he has been overwhelmed by the sheer volume of data he has amassed and catalogued.'

The walking and talking had exhausted him, and Ray helped him back into the farmhouse.

TWENTY-EIGHT

'We need to discuss this in private at my headquarters, Morris, since Brint here doesn't appear to have the slightest clue what we're on about,' Major General Phillips observed, adding, 'and this place is wrecked.'

Morris was now sufficiently calmed to be able to feel ashamed of his 'lily-livered' conduct and his shaking hands and lower jaw. For now, at the time of testing, he had 'text-book' frozen. He'd failed to be a man!

In fact, he was a... a coward. That was such an ignominious and disgusting term to employ to describe oneself. What an absolutely disgraceful, degrading shock!

Before this afternoon, Morris had always imagined that, under extreme, testing conditions, he would bring all the powers of that impressive intellect he possessed, and that others admired and envied, into play. That he would be able to look danger in the face resolutely and behave logically, according to the dictates of reason.

He had been called 'cold and distant' by his own wife, for God's sake! And he was kind of ashamed and proud at the same time when she had accused him. Of course, she was hardly the warmest of personalities herself! And, anyway, what the hell role had emotions got to play in his life? You didn't 'feel' your way into a new theory. You didn't 'emote' until the parameters of a hypothesis became apparent.

Granted that the term 'Prisoner 501', for example, might seem a trifle... impersonal, but to Morris, who was the only one who had created and understood its origin, it was perfectly logical. The '5' equated to a 'Close Encounter of the Fifth Kind', a UFO event that involved direct communication between aliens and humans. '01' indicated that the subject was possibly the first of its kind.

Agreed, it was hardly 'warm and cuddly', but then emotions were a damnable nuisance most of the time and had certainly had no role to play in research. Frustration was a positive blockage to creative thinking; anger, an irrational hindrance to introspective reflection! As for sadness, that was often the feeble response from pathetic types who indulged themselves in emotional 'porn' – people who positively enjoyed wallowing in misery!

And love... Really and truthfully, what was that, when you came to analyse it? Some kind of loose definition or rationale for basic, instinctive, sexual or cultural attraction!

And yet... And yet... He'd collapsed in a life-threatening moment of crisis. And feelings were what had done for him. How extraordinary!

'Morris?' Phillips had called, conscious that his interviewee had temporarily gone AWOL and was off in some alternative stream of consciousness. 'Are you ready?'

Morris, like a dog that had been clubbed into submission, trotted obediently behind Phillips down the corridor to the wrecked reception entrance. Soldiers appeared to be measuring the distance from where the entrance had been to the interrogation room, God alone knew why!

The clouds had temporarily cleared and the first thing they found, a hundred or so metres from the entrance steps, in sparkling sunshine, was a massive Boxer armoured vehicle lying on its back, as useful and vulnerable as an upturned turtle. Medics were still treating the occupants sitting on the ground around it. Funny, Morris heard jokes and banter being exchanged between the casualties and their helpers. How weirdly inappropriate was that!

As the professor trudged onwards behind Phillips towards Base HQ, the environment around him looked totally alien! At 8.00am that morning he had walked through the barracks towards Building 7 in a steady stream of rain and blustery winds. It had looked and felt a bit depressing, but it certainly seemed reassuringly 'conventional', whatever the hell that now was! Currently, he was walking through a landscape that bore little connection to normality.

The last of the casualties were being transported to the overflowing infirmary and it was really odd, but it was the simple things that threw you. A rose bed, always maintained to strict, military standards, now crushed and churned up by the slew of heavy-duty tyres. A post box warped and depressed into tarmac. A soldier's helmet, pancake flattened!

God! How many had died? How much his fault?

'You want a tea or coffee, Morris?' Phillips asked, almost kindly, as they walked into the commander's office.

'Sorry?' Morris asked, like a man who'd just emerged from a heavy nightmare.

'A drink, Morris? Do you want a tea or something stronger?'

'Yes… Yes, coffee would be good.'

Phillips sat down and studied his confused, distracted 'adversary'.

He knew exactly what Morris was feeling. Exactly!

All those years ago in the Gulf War he'd felt precisely the same; that first time a rocket launcher had been fired right next to him. He'd been lying on the ground, his eyes tight shut, trying to will them open so that he could, at least, discharge his weapon at something resembling an enemy. But the punch of bullets into the walls around him…

He kept anticipating one hitting right between his eyes, smashing his skull to fragments and spreading his brains across his comrades' battledress. Then the rocket launcher brought up, unknown to him, to take out the upper storey of the building opposite, had fired off! The noise was nerve-shockingly appalling!

Something had happened in his combat trousers. They suddenly felt comfortingly warm and wet; but they also stank.

The sheer, sheer, ignominious shame of it all! Fergus Mackenzie, an awkward lance corporal who'd always intimidated him, had been amazing. Told him how to get rid of the offensive garment and reassured him that he wouldn't be the first or last to have it happen. Absolutely terrific guy, who had lost most of his right leg three weeks later in a 'friendly fire' incident.

Less than a month after his shame, Lieutenant Phillips had happened to be in the right place at the right time. The enemy had wandered into the trap as if on some kind of picnic and his men had decimated them. He had found himself on an upwards trajectory based on one lucky action, and that trajectory had never faltered once since! Phillips, the courageous military genius, had been born that day, and every action he had done since had been judged in that warm and admiring light!

He felt sorry for Morris even as he felt contempt for his arrogance. Unfortunately, in his experience, 'sorry' didn't work half as well as cold, calculated terror.

'Right, Morris,' he started, 'you'd better tell me everything you know, because you're in serious, serious trouble, man.'

Morris had just felt mightily relieved and grateful that the man before him hadn't spat his contempt right in his face!

TWENTY-NINE

Ray listened intently; was that a vehicle coming down the track? He peered cautiously out to see his uncle drawing up in a Citroën saloon with Warrington in the passenger seat.

'Here,' Leary said, as he entered the building and threw a pile of clothing towards Ray and the Companion, 'help him get that lot on.'

In answer to Ray's look of enquiry Leary said, 'I got 'em in a charity shop. Don't ask where the car come from.'

The clothes were an old flower-patterned dress, cardigan, woman's overcoat and headscarf.

'You can't make him wear these!' Ray protested, outraged that a visitor from another world should be treated in such humiliating fashion.

'Listen, boy, they're looking for a middle-aged man, right? If I thought I could pull it off, I'd stick a tyre up his jacksie and pass him off as Kim Kardashian.'

Leary also threw over a lipstick and face compact. 'I

got these an' all. Make him up and don't get too fancy! I ain't planning on honeymooning with the beggar.'

He and Warrington went back outside.

Ray began to apologise to the Companion, who smiled at him and shook his head. 'It has been both fascinating and more than a little dispiriting, Raymond, to see how obsessed your species is with gender. It seems totally extraordinary that someone's sexuality could be a source of comment, friction or conflict!

'When I witness such violent reactions as to whether one human possesses a particular type of genitalia, or does not, and what that therefore entitles them to in your societies, or with what garments they cover their nakedness, I appreciate anew what a profoundly serious threat my companions and I represent, as *truly* alien beings.

'You appear to have an in-built terror of, and hostility towards, anything that looks or behaves differently to your tribe, whatever that is at the time. We are most certainly in deadly danger. So, if these materials camouflage and protect me, how could I possibly be distressed by such a, literally, superficial issue?'

Ray helped the Companion to remove the orange overall he was wearing, which confirmed what he had suspected. The Companion was no machine. He was genuine flesh and bone; he had to be. He was emaciated and had cuts, needle marks and bruises across his body, arms and legs.

Ray applied the makeup clumsily. Fortunately, the headscarf would cover much of the Companion's face. From a distance and through a windscreen, he might pass as a very vain, old woman.

Leary and Warrington came in to check out the final product. Leary looked the Companion up and down critically.

'Well, he ain't goin' to win any glamorous granny contests, is he?' he finally said.

'He looks awful!' Warrington observed.

'There you go! No proposals from Jonas then', said Leary. 'Your bum's safe, Kim. Jonas is a bottom-pincher, ain't you?'

'Oh, why don't you just belt up for once, Leary, before I give you one!' Warrington threatened, his fist clenching.

'See, I was wrong. A proposal already.' He checked his watch. 'Right, it's five twenty-four. Okay. A slow drive back'll take us to about half-six or thereabouts. I can book us in a hotel, somewhere close. We can hide out, get a bite to eat and then make that rendezvous. I'm phoning ahead. Wait here.'

He walked up the track to get a better phone signal and came back down minutes later.

'Okay. Let's get going.'

As they walked slowly up to the car, the Companion leaning against Ray for support, Leary lifted the boot lid.

'Right, Warrington,' he said, 'in you get.'

'You what!' Warrington demanded angrily. 'I'm not travelling twenty-odd miles in no boot.'

'Blood and sand, Warrington!' Leary exclaimed, looking up at the sky. 'What exactly are you bringing to this "partnership"? It certainly ain't guts, and if it's brains, I been short-changed. Come to think of it, so have you.'

'Listen, you—' began Warrington.

'No! You listen, pal! If anyone did get a shufti of us going to Derringham they'll be looking for four people at least, right? Truman should be drawing off most of 'em, but we can't take no chances. A gran, her son and grandson won't look too suspicious and that's why the boy here's going to sit up front. You, with that yard brush stuck under your hooter, look every inch ex-military. What's more, Warrington, I don't trust your acting skills if we do get stopped.'

'I'll suffocate in there!'

'It's a car boot, not a ruddy Tupperware box! Tell you what, you can "retain your anonymity" in there. You'd like that, wouldn't you?'

'Honestly, Leary, I'm telling you when this is all over—'

'Yeah. Yeah. Sure, Jonas. Now shut up and get in!' Leary ordered.

Warrington climbed carefully into the boot and lay in a foetal position, his knees almost up to his chin.

'Bit of practice for solitary confinement,' Leary observed, reaching for the boot lid.

Warrington went to get up and say something, but Leary pushed the lid shut.

'It's pitch dark in here!' Warrington's muffled voice protested.

'Well, there's a surprise. And the forecast said it was going to be bright and sunny all day,' Leary called.

Muffled swearing arose from the boot.

'Well, he seems happy enough,' Leary remarked.

Ray had got in the front passenger seat whilst the Companion sat in the back. Leary got into the car, belted himself up and turned the ignition.

'You all set, Kimmy?' he asked, looking in his mirror at the Companion who nodded. 'Right then.'

They drove up the track, apparently aiming for all the potholes and bumps.

Leary turned to Ray and winked. 'A "Warrington cocktail on the rocks". Shaken and definitely stirred,' he said, smiling broadly.

THIRTY

It was late afternoon and Professor Peter Morris's hands and jaw would still not stop trembling as he stumbled across the crunching shards of glass and twisted metal littering, what had previously been Building 7's reception area. He had returned, in vain, to retrieve his laptop following a two-hour interrogation with Major General Phillips – the last thing his shattered nerves had needed. The laptop contained some appalling evidence of possible malpractice on his and the team's part.

Despite his frequent and feeble protests that Phillip Faulkner, Director for Homeland Security, be contacted before he spoke further on the subject of the 'alien', Phillips had simply bulldozed through his objections.

Morris, usually so cool and in control, had found himself stumbling over his answers. He was traumatised, and he knew that suited Phillips' purpose just fine.

He was also in deep, deep trouble on many fronts. In five months of intensive research, he and his team had learnt virtually nothing about the alien's background and origins. His superior, being less than impressed with his performance, had led him to adopt measures towards the creature which were on the very knife edge between 'intensive investigation' and 'torture'.

He knew he had contravened the United Nations' Charter on Human Rights many, many times. But then it had no role at all to play in animal research and vivisection, had it? And since this had turned out to be no 'human' he'd been researching, there was more than a fair chance that the distinction might be sufficient to clear him of any wrongdoing!

But, added to that, for a distinguished scientist obsessed with discovering the 'truth' in phenomena, he had been lying continuously to his research team, Major General Phillips, his original employer who had seconded him grudgingly to this project, and other colleagues in genome research. The strain of maintaining the secrecy had been pretty well intolerable.

He reached the hire car in which he would be driving home to St Kitteridge. His brand-new Mercedes sports car, with the deeply dented bonnet and spread-eagled front wheels, was being lifted onto a transporter at that moment before its final destination at the scrapyard.

'Apparently, they're heading towards Westbourne at this moment,' Phillips read from a report just handed him. 'Any recommendations, Professor?'

Morris, momentarily heartened that his opinion was being sought, made a strenuous effort to regain some of his composure and authority.

'Well... well, throughout our research we found no indications of any hostility or aggression. My recommendation would be to track them and find an opportunity to negotiate, if possible. I'd… I'd be more than happy to undertake that role.'

'Well, that's really marvellous of you, Morris!' Phillips had replied witheringly. 'You've had getting on six months to "negotiate" with one of them, and I've now got two of the bloody things blundering through the highways and by-ways of Devon, heading towards a densely populated town. Two, Professor! If it's okay with you, I think I'll let my weaponry do the negotiation with them from this point on.'

'I think that would be a serious mistake,' Morris had advised.

'A very interesting point of view, Morris, on which you can no doubt elaborate at the Board of Inquiry to examine your handling of this affair. That's assuming we're all still alive and kicking by then. Be back here by seven tomorrow morning. Oh, and in the meantime, do me a real favour, will you, Morris?'

'Of course,' Morris replied eagerly, sensing there might be some opportunity, no matter how small, to redeem himself in the man's eyes.

'Just get out of my sight!'

THIRTY-ONE

It was raining hard again as they drove along quiet country roads, passing only the occasional vehicle. They stopped back at The Admiral pub to retrieve Warrington's car and abandon the Citroën. There seemed to be no sign of CCTV cameras, but they took no chances and kept their heads lowered as they exchanged vehicles.

Warrington, emerging from the boot, was red in the face, sweating and in the filthiest of tempers. Being expected to climb into the boot of his own car felt like almost one insult too many for him. At least he'd been able to tell Leary where the switch for the internal light was.

The Companion said nothing on the journey, just sat looking ill and bemused. Looking at him in a headscarf and with smudged lipstick, Ray felt that his humiliation at the base was merely continuing in a different guise.

Ray would have liked to be able to say how refined and dignified the Alien-Companion appeared, but it was hard for any creature to do that when they looked such a complete twerp. The Companion didn't seem remotely concerned about his appearance, but Ray still was. A 'being from another world' should look the Hollywood part, and not resemble a third-rate drag act!

An army vehicle had passed them a few miles outside the town, travelling in the opposite direction, but they were not stopped. It was just after 6.40pm when they drove back into Brookdale-on-Sea as the light was starting to fade.

Ray felt that his own little world had simply changed entirely and forever. He couldn't recall what it felt like to feel 'normal'. He was already going to be in hot water with his mother for being late, but what did that kind of nonsense matter in the face of something as huge as this?

Leary pulled up at the hotel and went inside alone. Emerging from it minutes later he assisted Ray in guiding the Companion to the family room he'd booked. He explained that he would drop Warrington back at his house before returning.

The Companion fell exhausted onto the double bed and, some forty minutes later, Leary returned with sandwiches, soft drinks and two double whiskies for himself. Ray showered and had never enjoyed the sensation so much. He was starting to feel human again.

The Companion just lay on the bed, immobile. Ray tried to get him to eat and drink something, but he was simply too ill and wearied to bother.

THIRTY-TWO

Warrington was leaning over the damaged car boot, puce in the face and gasping.

'Can you hear me, Warrington?' Leary had hissed at the boot an hour and a half ago. 'We're outside the flat and there's a group of kids hanging round. Zita's mate has left some stuff hidden here he needs.'

'What did we stop for earlier?' Warrington called.

'For God's sake, keep your bloody voice down! The kids'll hear you! We won't be more than thirty or forty minutes. Now lie still!'

Warrington swore and then went quiet.

It had taken him over fifty minutes to realise that something was drastically wrong and a further forty to get the boot of the car open. He had heard the distant sound of vehicles, not appreciating that one of them was the taxi that Leary had arranged at the deserted farmhouse to be picked up by.

His breathing becoming less frantic, he finally looked up about him, befuddled.

'*Welcome to Astor Country Park*' the sign in the deserted car park read.

Ten miles out from Brookdale-on-Sea, no keys to his own car, not a person in sight and Lord knew how far to walk before he got a signal for his mobile!

Leary had lied to him! He'd taken the Companion! He'd welched on the deal!

He was dead!

*

Twenty minutes later and a few hundred metres from the hotel, Gerald Dunstable sat at his desk, a knot in the pit of his stomach, unable to concentrate. He and Stapleton had spent another exhausting afternoon in videoconference with Francis R. Petersen, who was still pressing for a takeover, or merger, with Vader International.

Vader himself was being kept carefully in the dark about the development. Petersen, the founder and CEO of the mighty Rococo Enterprises, had grown the business from three geek student pals playing around with mainframes in a garage in Santa Monica, into one of the six top digital companies on the planet. He had 'lost', or perhaps it could more accurately be described as 'cast aside', his two buddies on the way.

He seemed to know far more about the new quantum processor than Dunstable or Stapleton had expected. Both men had felt distinctly out of their depth in the negotiations as he proposed again sharing the research with extremely tempting terms for Vader International.

Dunstable had felt flattered, but the man's pushiness had made him uneasy, and he had resisted the proposal. If Petersen were this interested in what Vader International was doing at this early stage in its development, Dunstable felt confident such offers of expansion would come pouring in from other companies once the processor was on the market.

The newsflash on the local channel about an incident at the Derringham Commando Training Barracks had shocked him.

'Mr Dunstable?' The intercom came on; Jenny, his secretary, had been working overtime preparing the party.

'Yes?'

'There's a call for you. The gentleman's saying it's urgent.'

'Well, who is it?' Dunstable asked irritably.

'He won't say, I'm afraid.'

'Put it through!'

Jenny Simmons pulled a face. She'd never known Mr Dunstable to be so abrupt and rude before.

His hand was trembling as he picked up the receiver. 'Where the hell have you been all this time…? Well, what the hell *is* going on? Listen, you were hired specifically to… Never mind about that! You never told me there was going to be… I know! There's a special report on the *Southwest News*… No! I said no! Just do what we agreed. And don't foul this up any more than you have already!'

He slammed the phone down and pressed the intercom. 'Get Manley on the line for me. I'll be up in Vader's suite. You can leave then.'

'Right, Mr Dunstable,' Miss Simmons said, pulling another face.

Mr Dunstable was in a right old mood tonight and no mistake, she thought.

Dunstable, releasing the intercom switch, lay back in his chair and ran his fingers through his thick hair. Things had been complicated enough before today's news had hit him like a steam shovel. Tonight was it! He sank or prospered on what happened this evening. There were now so many possible variations to his plans, his head was spinning. He took a deep breath and made his way through the secretary's office. The woman was starting to pack away her things and clear her desk ready for home, before placing the call.

'Goodnight, Mr Dunstable!' she called out brightly as he headed for the lift.

He didn't answer. She shrugged her shoulders. It had been 'one of those days'.

THIRTY-THREE

Ray, resting on the bed, looked across at the Companion, snoring slightly. His uncle had said he was going down to get himself another double Scotch. When he returned, he had switched on the television.

The *Southwest News* led with a photo of the Companion, similar to the passport one his uncle had given Ray less than a week ago. This one looked more like one of those official photos police take, following an arrest.

A week ago! How much had changed for Ray in that time!

The newsreader's voice came over the picture. 'Following our earlier report of a serious incident during a training exercise at the Derringham Commando Training Barracks, the authorities have now released a picture of one of the two people they wish to interview. The man, described as being around five-eleven in height and in his fifties, has a history of serious mental illness. Police have said he is extremely dangerous, and the public are warned not to approach him.

'The authorities have still not confirmed what happened earlier today, but roads to and from the base have been closed and diversions are causing major congestion in the area.

'In other news from the region, Emergency Services have been called to Westbourne following reports of a...'

Ray looked over at the Companion, his makeup smudged, his lipstick-smeared mouth slightly open: '*extremely dangerous*'!

'Jesus!' said Leary pulling on his shoes and shaking the Companion.

'Come on, boy!' he urged Ray.

He hustled them out of the room, down the corridor to the fire escape. The Companion was stumbling, and Ray did what he could to support him.

'What is happening?' the Companion asked, bewildered.

'There's been a change of plan, cock. If anyone got a gander at you, this place'll be swarming with coppers and soldiers in about two minutes,' Leary replied.

'I need to rest a little longer,' the Companion protested.

'Yeah, well you can have all the rest you want when you're dead, pal! And that ain't going to be too far off unless you move yourself. Pronto!'

'Isn't Mr Warrington coming?' Ray asked.

'Yeah... Probably not, son. Busy with his own stuff I should think.'

Leary half pushed, half supported the Companion down the metal stairs. Once out in the road they kept to the shadows as much as possible. The Companion moved slowly but Leary drove him forward with a zeal Ray had never suspected he possessed. He did more genuine work in the quarter-hour it took to get to the Vader offices than he had done in all the time Ray had known him, at one point carrying the Companion across his shoulders.

Finally, they arrived. Only the top floor of the building was lit up; the rest was in darkness. Leary looked carefully up and down the road, which seemed deserted.

'Come on!' he urged.

As they came up the front steps a figure emerged from the shadows around the corner. A torrent of abuse directed at Leary was followed by Warrington grabbing him by the front of his jacket. They struggled but were quickly pulled apart by men who came running out from somewhere in reception.

One grabbed Ray and forced his arm up his back while the others did the same to Leary and the Companion, and two men subdued Warrington. Ray involuntarily let out a cry with the pain and felt embarrassed by how unmanly it sounded. They hustled them through the reception area and into the lift. Manley, standing at the side, stepped in with them and stood staring into Leary's face.

'Hello, toe rag,' he said, beaming and clearly relishing the moment. 'Why don't you give us one of your funnies?'

Then he slapped him hard across the face.

'You're making a big mistake,' Leary said, surprisingly calm.

'Yeah? Yeah, sure I am. We can have that little visit to my fairground you made such a smart crack about. I can tell you now though, tough guy, you ain't going to feel much like laughing after it,' Manley said with a wide smile.

'Funny, Charlie. Do you know, that's exactly what I hear most of your fairground punters say?' replied Leary.

Manley snorted. 'Yeah, you go right ahead, Leary. Wind me up. Just keep making it tougher on yourself, feller, 'cos I'm really going to enjoy this.'

The lift stopped at the top floor and the doors slid back to reveal a large, luxurious office which stretched across most of the floor of the building. There was an area with a Chesterfield sofa, leather easy chairs and coffee table, and in the window a conference table with an enormous buffet and drinks set across it.

The whole of one wall was mirrored like a dance studio. On the wall opposite was a huge desk with a large, elegant reading lamp and two computers. To the left was a door leading to a private room. A figure Ray couldn't make out was seated behind the desk, the lamp obscuring his face. Standing beside him was Dunstable, trying to look as smart and cool as ever.

He came from behind the desk and advanced, smiling at them.

'Do let them go, gentlemen,' he said to Manley's men.

The Companion slumped to his knees as he was released.

'Well done! Really, excellent, excellent work!' Dunstable said.

Ray looked with disgust at Warrington.

'I just knew you were the right man for the job,' Dunstable continued, and then took hold of and shook... his uncle's hand!

THIRTY-FOUR

'So, when exactly were you people going to tell the rest of us about this bloody alien?' Major General Phillips demanded of Faulkner, gripping the scrambled telephone angrily in his fist, whilst cursorily looking at the reports still arriving on his desk.

'Major General Phillips, you are not following protocol. Professor Morris had no business to be talking about this issue with you. We are very clear that—' the voice down the line began.

'Blast your protocol, Faulkner! I'm sitting in the middle of a bloody warzone here and you're spouting rubbish about protocol! I've got a base that looks like Basra, twenty-six injured personnel when it could have been up to a couple of hundred dead, and it turns out that an idiot boffin you've borrowed off some corporation knows a whole lot more about it than I do! I'm a NATO commander, for Christ's sake! What the hell do you think you're playing at, man?'

'You're stepping well over your authority here, Phillips. I suggest you calm yourself and leave the matter with me.'

'Calm myself?! Really? You'd just like me to hang around until this "thing", whatever the hell it is, decides to toddle back for another visit. Is that it?'

'Listen, Phillips, we're pretty certain this was a one-off incursion.'

'Really? "Pretty certain"? Well, I tell you what, old man, "pretty certain" just isn't bloody certain enough! Why don't you get off your backside up there in the safety of Whitehall and pay us a little visit down here? My forces have been trailing and blasting away at this thing for the past half-hour.'

'"Blasting away"! What the hell does that mean?' Faulkner demanded.

'It means, Director Faulkner, that when my base gets attacked by a hostile force, I don't sit around waiting for it to come back!'

'Christ! What collateral damage has there been?' Faulkner was sounding furious.

'By "collateral" I presume you mean civilian? None. They only fired at it in open ground.'

'The whole of bloody Devon must have heard you!'

'Well, I'm terribly sorry if my men have been noisy and indiscreet. They tend to get like that when they're ambushed.'

'I'm finishing this conversation now, Major General, before one of us says something we'll regret.'

'I haven't even started yet, Director. I'm going—'

The line went dead, and Phillips looked at the receiver murderously before throwing it onto the desk.

THIRTY-FIVE

It took Ray a full three seconds to register the significance of what had just happened and even then, he couldn't quite believe it.

A limp 'Uncle Garry?' was all he could muster.

Leary looked down for a moment and then up, his eyes livid with rage. 'Don't give me any of your lip, sunshine! I told you. I know what I'm doing!'

'How long?' was all Ray could manage.

'How long has he been working for me?' Dunstable interjected. 'Since just after his little drug-arrest problem, actually.

'Yes, Charles,' he continued, for Manley looked as flummoxed as Ray and Warrington at the turn of events, 'Garry and I came to a little arrangement. He's a very, very astute man actually, aren't you, Garry? He remembers how unpleasant incarceration can be and I happen to have connections on the magistrates' bench. I can pretty well guarantee him a suspended sentence with some hours of community service, as regards the drug offences. And, on top of that, he does so like his "cash", doesn't he?

'I have to say, Charles,' he continued, 'we were both rather upset about you having arranged that little brawl; him rather more than me, not surprisingly. I did ask you to leave matters to me, didn't I? Violence in public always draws attention and you should know by now how very, very keen I am to avoid that.'

Manley looked uncomfortable and annoyed, as if he were the hard, naughty kid being disciplined in front of the class.

'But since then,' continued Dunstable, 'we've had the most marvellous working relationship, haven't we, Garry? You should be very, very proud of your uncle, young man,' he said, turning to Ray, 'he's no *loser*. He's a man who knows what he wants and goes for it!'

Ray could sense Leary looking intently at him but couldn't trust himself to return the gaze. Uncle Garry, he thought, was precisely what Dunstable had called him in his office that day: 'sleazy, squalid and third rate.' Only a lot more so!

Two of Manley's men had helped the Companion over to the sofa and Dunstable approached him.

'Well, well, whatever have we here?' Dunstable asked, scanning the Companion's bizarre clothing and makeup. 'Old Mother Riley no less.'

'Gerald!' called the figure behind the desk.

Dunstable briefly lost his smile and turned to Manley. 'Right. We have some very complicated business to go through now, and Mr Vader would like a word with these gentlemen in private, Charles.'

He indicated the lift. 'Please excuse us. Keep Warrington on hold for the time being, will you? We'll sort that particular problem out later,' he said to Manley, who looked furious at being dismissed.

Warrington turned to Leary. 'You're the scrapings at the bottom of the barrel, aren't you, Leary? I've never had much of an opinion of meself, but next to you... I'm a bloody hero.'

'Listen, Warrington,' Leary said, 'if you'd stayed put where I left you, none of this would be happening. I'd have come back for you later and sorted things.'

'Yeah. Sure, Leary. You just keep pretending for the sake of the boy there. I'm dead sorry for you, son. That's some stinking uncle you got.'

Warrington was manhandled into the lift, surrounded by Manley and his men. The doors closed and the lift descended.

The Companion had been straining his eyes across the room ever since the figure behind the desk had spoken.

'Is that you?' he finally asked.

There was no reply, but the figure stood up and Ray gasped, for probably the first time in his life, with surprise. It was like seeing each of the two Trumans in over-ripe technicolour. This one had the same bland, middle-aged features but a full head of thick, blond hair. His complexion was an orange tan, his eyes unnaturally bright, his teeth gleaming white and the expression on his face sophisticated and superior. He was dressed in a very expensive, blue, shiny silk suit which was too fashionably young for his age. As he spoke, he kept admiring his appearance in the wall-to-wall mirror.

'How absolutely, exquisitely wonderful to meet you all at last!' he began, in refined, plummy tones. 'Ah, and you must be "the boy"', he said, turning to Ray with a smile and leaning in towards him. 'Tell me, what's your function in life?'

'Sorry?' Ray asked, puzzled.

'What do you do for a living?' Vader elaborated, tilting his head to look intently and sincerely into Ray's eyes.

'Oh. I'm… I'm at school.'

'Really? How marvellously interesting! And what do you do there exactly?' Vader asked, apparently fascinated.

'Well, I… I'm studying for exams. I'm doing English and literature, science, some—'

'Science? Do tell more.'

'Well, it's er… It's kind of a mix of biology, chemistry and physics. Er, the teacher… Well, it's three really, but Mr Rogers takes most of the classes, and we're following this course where you—'

Vader was nodding vigorously and mumbling encouragement all the while Ray was speaking. 'Um. Yes. Um. Fascinating. Yes. Yes. Uh-huh. Yah. Mesmerising. Yes. Yeah. Yeah. Yeah. Yeah. Yeah. Yeah. Yeah. Yah. Yah. Yah…

'Actually, no!' he suddenly interrupted. 'No, I really am going to have to stop you there, I'm afraid. I've just realised you're not important at all, and I'm finding both you and this conversation terribly, terribly tedious.'

He turned to Leary, his back to Ray.

'Ah, so, we finally meet at last. You must be the Great Garry. Garrrrry.' He trilled out the 'r'.

'Gerald's talked ever so much about you! Such a riveting, riveting, deep, deep, wondrous personality! He said you were er… What was it you said, Gerald? Oh, yes! He said you could be jolly, jolly useful to our organisation. He went on to suggest that you might be an "oik", with a body odour problem connected with your smoking and lifestyle, before adding—'

'Ian!' Dunstable's tone of voice stopped Vader dead.

Vader looked momentarily confused and turned back to Ray. 'Oh dear! Did I just make another social gaffe there? I'm very pained by that. I'm still learning, you see. Gerald's very clever about these things and puts me right when I get them wrong. I don't always understand it, because Gerald is just as charming as can be when he meets people, and then says the most appalling things about them behind their backs.'

'Ian!' Dunstable warned again.

'Oh no! Have I done it again?' Vader asked, shaking his head woefully.

He turned back to Leary. 'I'm awfully, awfully sorry, Garrrrry. Gerald said you could be jolly, jolly useful and that you were also a very, very, very, very, very, very, very, very nice and very pleasantly fragranced fellow! Did I get that right, Gerald?'

'Listen, Dunstable, I've had a really hard day and I want to get the lad home,' Leary called across the room. 'I ain't got the time to stand round listening to rubbish.'

'Make time!' Dunstable replied.

Vader turned to Ray. He suddenly seemed to have given the role of confidant to him, though Ray had no idea why.

'That wasn't very nice, was it, what that Garry person just said?'

He turned back to Leary. 'That was rude. I'm beginning to think...'

He broke off, searching for the right words. 'I'm beginning to think you might actually be a little, short-arse, smelly crud. Gerald certainly described you in some such terms.'

'Listen, you!' Leary began, advancing towards Vader, who neatly placed himself behind Dunstable.

'Gerald, if that chappie takes one more step towards me, I shan't be responsible for my actions. Please warn him that, as a sporting man, I happen to be a black belt, thirty-third Dan on the Devon County Kung Fu Video-Game League. I have over 283 "kills" to my name.'

'Leary!' Dunstable, feeling unusually irritable, called. 'For God's sake, get a grip, man!'

Leary stopped, muttered something about 'headcases' and sat down next to the sofa where the Companion was lying.

For the first time Vader seemed to become aware of the Companion's presence. He walked across and looked him up and down coldly.

'You look... just... ridiculous!' he spat out angrily and with disgust and then, with an abrupt change of mood, called cheerily to Dunstable, 'Now those dreadful people have gone, I believe it's time for my party, Gerald. I'll have one of those big drinks with those little umbrella thingies in them!'

Dunstable went to say something, thought better of it, and went across to the drink's cabinet.

'Well,' said Vader, rubbing his hands together gleefully, 'I believe the function of a party, and indeed all human activity here, is to have as much fun as possible. I've done intensive research into the merry-making, revelry and general hi-jinks that characterise such social interactions. Discovered Étoile and just adored Hannah Mendelsohn's aristocratic take on the ritual. So, I believe I can say, with the greatest possible confidence, that you're all in for a heady mix of fun, glee and mind-blowing surprises. Literally, mind-blowing!'

He pulled a single, small party popper from his pocket and shot the streamers at Leary, Ray and the Companion. They landed and hung over the Companion's headscarf and forehead, strangely adding to his mournful appearance.

'What has happened to you?!' the Companion asked, sounding and looking astonished at his colleague's behaviour.

'Oh! Lots and lots!' cried Vader. 'But come on. Everybody sit down and listen to me, because this is my party and I'm obviously the centre of attention!'

Leary snorted in frustrated disgust. Ray sat in one of the easy chairs, as far from his uncle as he could.

'Come on, Gerald!' Vader called.

'I'll sit over here, Ian, at the desk. I've got work to do. You've got exactly an hour and then we'll have to discuss business.'

'He's spoiling the party, isn't he?' Vader observed to Ray.

He dropped the volume of his voice so only Ray could hear the next part. 'I actually think he's a big-headed smelly, and I really hate him and wish he would die soon.'

Then he flashed a wide grin across at Dunstable. 'I just love him to bits!' he announced to the room in general.

Ray was utterly bewildered by Vader's wildly unpredictable swings of mood from pompous arrogance to mindless cheerfulness to heartfelt viciousness. It was like standing in the middle of an 'emotional hurricane'.

'Tell me, Garry, are you having just the most enormous fun at my party?' Vader asked Leary solicitously, apparently having forgotten the incident of a few moments before.

'Oh yeah, sure, pal. Haven't had this much fun since I dropped a crate of brown ale on me toe.'

'*Really?!* Which foot?' Vader asked, fascinated.

'Ian!' Dunstable warned.

'Left, now I come to think on it. You want to try it sometime, pal,' Leary suggested.

'Any particular make of ale?' Vader asked earnestly.

'Well, for you, chummy, "Old Peculier" should do the—'

'Now, Ian, let's not start all that again!' Dunstable interrupted angrily, remembering the last incident involving the hammer, nails and religious picture. 'If I hadn't come in when I did, Lord knows what injuries you would have done to yourself!'

'Yes, but then that's just so typical of you, Gerald, isn't it! Always spoiling my fun! You have no comprehension at all how narrow the dividing line between excruciating agony and exquisite pleasure is here. It's all so ridiculously relative.'

He turned to Ray again. 'As I said, I do know you're supposed to have the most enormous fun here all the time, which is why I had these party games planned. But, do you know, I still can't quite figure out where the "fun" element actually is!

'"Pin the tail back on the donkey" was one. Now, I researched the surgical procedures required for the initial amputation of the tail, but then discovered it's going to take literally hours to stitch it back on, blindfold. I mean I welcome a challenge as much as the next person, but why a blindfold? Why not have to wear handcuffs if you're looking to handicap people?'

'Ian!' Dunstable called.

'And if you fail to suture up the complex nerve tissues correctly, well, the tail's going to be quite useless anyway. That's why I was looking at the possibility of replacing it with a small, solar-powered windmill affair to drive the flies off the donkey's, you know... "bottie". I've been studying veterinary in-house magazines.'

'Ian,' Dunstable called again.

'And I've got the designs for it here somewhere. Gerald! Where's my "Fan-the-flies-off-the-donkey's-bottie" project? It was next to my "Pass-the-suspicious-looking-parcel" game. Of course, *he* wouldn't let me have the Semtex explosives for that one, would he! Too "*dangerous*" apparently. Absolutely typical!' Vader said in an angry aside to Ray.

'Ian,' Dunstable enunciated wearily, 'please, please just calm down and try to listen. It's not a real donkey. It's a drawing. You leave the tail off and draw others for people to pin them back on with.'

Vader's relentless drivel had a way of getting inside your head, Dunstable reflected; he was just so loud and incessantly demanding!

'Oh!' Vader said, sounding disappointed. 'Well, why draw it without a tail? Why not leave an ear off? Or a nostril. I tell you what, you could do an anatomical drawing and leave one of the kneecaps off.'

'Honestly, Ian, it really doesn't matter what part you leave off.'

'Well, it would to the donkey. If it had no kneecap, it would fall over.'

'Please, Ian! It really, really doesn't matter! Now, will you please, please leave the donkey issue alone. Please!'

Dunstable ran his hands through his hair, a man at the end of his tether. He forced a smile onto his face.

'Look, Ian, shall I get you some more of your medication?' he asked.

'No, Margaret's already dosed me up! There she is, a Christian teetotaller and anti-recreational drugs campaigner, and she just keeps on shoving these tranquillisers down my neck all day. There's got to be a contradiction there, surely!

'She suggested Charades as a game but when I looked it up, it said, "Fakes, shams and make-believes". And, as far as I can tell, everybody's being or doing that all the time here anyway. Margaret is, certainly!

'I did think of doing "Harakiri-aoke". It's my version of a sing-along. Somebody, with the usual absence of any musical talent, sings at everybody else but this time they all disembowel themselves while he's doing it, because it's just so appallingly embarrassing and excruciating to watch… But that doesn't really seem like a very "fun" way to pass the time, does it?'

'Ian!' Dunstable warned.

'I tell you what, "the boy", Vader began to chortle, 'how about… How about Trivial Pursuit? No! No! We can't play that!'

Here Vader paused, his mirth preventing further explanation.

'And I'll tell you why!' he snorted triumphantly. 'That's not fun! That's just a definition of everyday living on this dump!'

He threw back his head, exploded with a guffaw and continued to laugh like a maniac. It was high-pitched and on the verge of hysterical. Dunstable sat forward, his elbows on the desk, his hands covering his ears. Leary and Ray stared open-mouthed. The Companion looked on sadly, his eyes glistening.

'Dear, oh dear, oh dear!' Vader said finally, as he wiped away his tears. 'I do so love a good old laugh, though, don't you? You spend so much time here trying to laugh away your problems rather than solving them. But then, of course, laughter is the best medicine and makes the world go around, doesn't it? I read that on a matchbox… Or was it penicillin and gravity? Do you know, I really can't remember?'

Ray was looking at him, utterly perplexed and alarmed.

'You're awfully serious, aren't you?' Vader suddenly accused him, petulantly. 'And a bit of a killjoy, really!'

'Look, I got to get this lad back to his mother,' Leary called across to Dunstable.

He saw no reason why Ray should be drawn into any more of this bizarre rubbish.

'Shut up,' Dunstable said, bored and not looking up from his paperwork.

'Yes! Shut up!' repeated Vader. 'Or you won't be one of my bestest ever friends anymore, Garrrrry.'

Leary shook his head incredulously. Vader suddenly struck his forehead with the heel of his hand.

'I know! I know what fun we can have! I've got it! You're going to love this, "the boy"! You really, really are!' Vader exclaimed. 'You too, Garrrry! How about this? It's an "Audience With". I've seen them on TV!' He paused dramatically, before announcing, 'An audience with, and all about... Me!

'Yes! Yes! I'm going to go through every tiny little thing that's happened to me over the past 293 days, twenty-one hours,' he checked his watch, 'and forty-seven minutes I've been here!

'I'll call it, "An Audience with Ian Vader and His Adventures in Funderland"!'

For a purely coincidental reason, Leary thought for a moment of his drinking partner, Jack Sunderland, down at the British Legion Club. He, and all the other men there, were more than happy to moan on about their wives, families, health, or their football team's troubles, without ever asking a single question of their listener. Vader wasn't really all that different.

'Gosh! I so wish I was you,' Vader continued seriously, 'I really, really do! Because I'm the "fun" gift that just keeps on giving, aren't I? Shall I start now? Shall I? If I start now, I could do it any number of times and multiply the fun!'

'Jeez!' Leary muttered, slumping in his seat.

Suddenly, Vader's Harakiri-aoke, suspicious-looking-parcel game and dropping a crate of brown ale on his foot didn't seem like such bad options.

THIRTY-SIX

'It's been taken out, sir,' Flight Lieutenant Simon Davis radioed in to Major General Phillips. 'Light and visibility were poor, so we had to move in at close range. It went clear off the cliff into the sea. We're approximately two miles north of Westbourne, hovering over the point. We've got Navy divers about to go into the area to confirm.'

'What was the delay? Did it offer any resistance?'

'None at all, sir. It wouldn't respond to our loudhailer requests, so we did as you ordered. There was a problem with the cameras and weaponry,' Davis lied, 'but our gunner hit it numerous times. I'm afraid there's debris from it and the van littering the immediate area. It's going to need clearing.'

'That's being arranged.'

'Do you want us to return to base?'

'No. Circle the area. A good two-mile radius. I want to know it's definitely been destroyed. Good work, Flight Lieutenant.'

'Where's Bomber, and what the hell was going on back there?' Davis asked his co-pilot, Jez Nichols, as he returned to his seat.

Bomber, their nickname for Gunner Flight Sergeant Andy Harris, was a thirty-seven-year-old veteran and should have known better!

'It's… it's a woman!' he'd called on the intercom when they had moved to within a couple of hundred metres of the target. 'You still want me to fire on it?'

'I don't give a damn what it looks like!' Davis had called back. 'That's the designated target and it's just attacked a military installation. Take it down, Bomber! Bomber! That's an order! Bomber!

'Get back there and find out what the hell the problem is!' Davis had ordered his co-pilot when no sound or vibration of gunfire had occurred.

He was drawing on his considerable skill as a pilot, moving at just fifteen metres above the ground in the twilight, whilst maintaining a distance of only fifty metres from the target. He was trying to hold the helicopter and its spotlight at an angle that would allow Harris optimum firepower. The cameras had failed again and, strain as he could, he was unable to see clearly across the cockpit through the co-pilot's window. Fumes from the engine, as a result of the angled flight, didn't help.

Harris had the minigun, a Gatling-type machinegun capable of 3,000 rounds per minute, pointing at the target as Nichols entered the main fuselage. It was still pushing the van, or what remained of it, towards the cliff edge at considerable speed.

'What's the problem, Bomber? Come on, man!'

Nichols' presence and words seemed to break Harris's almost hypnotised spell. He opened fire at the receding back, the body of the vehicle shredding into a latticework of white, metal lace. The cliff edge seemed to be approaching rapidly and the target gave one last, lunging shove to the vehicle, before it dug its heels and feet in the ground at a ninety-degree angle, like a skier coming to a halt. The van sailed over the edge, only beginning to somersault downwards some seven metres away.

Harris's finger eased off the trigger. The target, a mere metre from the cliff edge, turned and stood looking up directly at the gunner.

'Take it down!' Davis's harsh voice, made even more robotic by the intercom's metallic tones, came loudly down the men's headsets. 'Take it down!'

Harris let his helmeted head fall on the gunsight. 'I… I can't…' he mumbled.

'What the hell's going on back there? Take it down! Nichols! Take it down!' Davis's voice called.

Nichols pushed the limp body of Harris aside. There was no resistance from him. He sighted up the target in the beam of light, surprised to find himself in a cold sweat. The ridiculously focused features of a middle-aged woman seemed to stare back into his eyes.

'Take the bloody thing down!' came out more like a shriek than a measured command from his superior.

Nichols fired at the body, which seemed to dance like a frenzied marionette. He saw a hand fly off, and involuntarily closed his eyes. The target staggered back under the ferocious hail of bullets. Its arms seemed to raise in surrender as it twisted and slowly toppled off the edge.

'Bomber's okay. Just a bit shaken up,' Jez Nichols reported minutes later as he strapped himself back in the co-pilot's chair.

His voice and hands were still shaky. 'It did look like a woman,' he added unnecessarily.

Bomber was currently sitting on the bench seat beside the minigun, his helmet off, his sweat-drenched head clasped between his hands.

'What the hell was it?' Nichols suddenly asked his skipper.

He was fervently hoping for an explanation that would clear him from feeling sickened and ashamed of what he had just done. For the woman had looked up at him calmly, steadily... almost kindly.

'It was a bloody cock-up! That's what it was, Jez! What the hell were you and Bomber playing at?'

His anger and anxiety diminishing, he could see and hear how upset his co-pilot was. 'Look, we'll all be signing D notices when we get back,' he continued, in an effort to restore some sense of detached calm to the situation. 'Which means we don't have to ever mention it again to a living soul. You heard the base. Let's check out the area one more time.'

Nichols felt a cold shudder come over him. Somewhere in his mind he knew that this incident today would become a seminal moment in his life. For the woman had smiled up at him, a millisecond before he pressed the firing mechanism.

The Wildcat helicopter banked and headed out to sea again.

THIRTY-SEVEN

Thirty-five minutes had elapsed since Vader had promised to tell of his 'adventures' and the intervening time had been filled with the most absurd antics by the man. He had suddenly decided that the shirt he was wearing was, 'all wrong and too white; and too wrong and all white'.

He had emerged from his bedroom, more times than Ray could count, wearing different shirts and ties of every colour of the rainbow it seemed.

'What do you think? What do you think?' he badgered a bored Dunstable and increasingly, as the fashion parade continued, an ever more bewildered Ray.

As he carefully studied his image in the wall mirror, he listened to none of Dunstable's wearied opinions but expressed his own series of bizarre appraisals of the outfits in overexcitable tones.

'No! It's just so… Magenta!

'Too Gerald on a bad day!

'Too good on a Gerald day!

'Makes me look like a frumpy, Freemason railway clerk at Sevenoaks!

'Oops! That's just too extremely Pope Francisishishishishish!

'OMG! It's simply not bronchial enough!

'Makes me look too fat, thin, tall, short, normal, abnormal, too normal!

'Far too sophisticated in a poo-poo, wee-wee, sicky-sicky kind of way!

'Now that is too, too, too Beyoncé!

'Not Beyoncé enough!'

And simply: 'Trump!'

Each of these rejections of each separate shirt and tie was preceded with him stating with total authority and certainty as he admired himself in the mirror, 'That's it! That's definitely, definitely *it*! That's the outfit! No doubt about it! Perfect in every detail! Fashionable! *A la mode!* Brilliant! Beautiful! Superb! Outstanding! Gorgeous! In fact, awesome!

'No! No! In fact, awful! Outdated! *Fin de siècle!* Dreadful! Appalling! Atrocious! A disgrace! Burn it!'

All the while, Leary sat, frustrated and ashamed. What box of frogs had he dragged poor Ray into? he thought. He heartily despised all the people he had thrown his lot in with – Dunstable, Manley and now this raving Vader lunatic. All nasty, egotistical scumbags!

Ray wouldn't even look at him now!

On three occasions he had caught Dunstable's attention and tapped his watch urgently, indicating his need to take Ray home and out of all this. Dunstable had simply looked down again at his work.

Finally, Vader had settled on his blue suit, now with a bulging pocket, a scarlet-red tie and bright-yellow shirt.

'What do you think? What do you think? What do you think?' he asked Dunstable, Ray and even Leary in turn.

'Absolutely you, Ian!' Dunstable had mouthed insincerely.

'Er… yeah,' Ray had mumbled with confusion and embarrassment.

'Perfect, pal,' Leary said, muttering when Vader had gone out of earshot to the other side of the room, 'for the circus, you colour-blind clown.'

'I'm ready!' he called out proudly.

He waved enthusiastically at them, then cleared his throat noisily. 'First of all, Lady and Gentlemen, I have to say, and I think you'd all agree, that I'm the cleverest, most talented and handsomest creature on this planet!' he paused before adding, 'And you're all nothing!'

He stopped and smiled with a look of real pleasure at his own superiority. Ray involuntarily caught his uncle's eye, who looked as bewildered at the direction this monologue was taking as Ray felt.

Vader went over to the table with the buffet on it, picked up a crystal glass, pinged it with his finger and then went and studied the bottles of wine arranged at the farthest end of the table.

'Ah, a 2017 Château Lafite Rothschild… To die for!' he declared to the group, uncorking the bottle, and pouring the ruby-red liquid into his glass.

'Ah, but there's a '97 Chablis, I espy!' he called, lifting the bottle from its ice bucket, raising it high into the air and studying its colour against the inset lighting above.

He pulled the cork and poured the golden liquor into another glass, swirling the red and white in each hand.

He sniffed deeply first at the Chablis. 'Such a delicately honeyed flavour with high notes of flint, and yet...' he raised the other glass to his nostrils, 'who can deny that brilliantly defined nose of black fruit, graphite and limestone? Simply electrifying in its intensity!

'I tell you, my friends, we should celebrate and revere the centuries of viniculture that have brought forth and metamorphosed that pulpy, fermented grape into an elixir of life itself. Remembering, of course, that the real question for all we wine connoisseurs, once you rip away the pretentious, pompous piffle, is which one will get me rat-arsed quickest?'

He drained both glasses together, one at each corner of his mouth, smacked his lips and moved over to the buffet end of the table, grabbing three of everything that were on the serving dishes, before standing where he could dominate the group. He appeared to swallow whole three canapés from his enormously heaped plate.

'Ummm! Absolutely delicious!' he said. 'I just can't get enough of them! Mind, they're murder on the waistline. Still, I work out every day. Cheryl says you should always aim to take two hours' exercise after each meal... Or is it instead of each meal? Anyway, I think she's just fabulous! She's my icon and inspiration! I keep myself in terrific shape, don't you think?'

He appraised his image in the mirror again.

'I really don't know why they chose to create these bodies. Something to do with not drawing attention to ourselves, "she" said. Still, I think I've done an absolutely fabulous job with the one I got!'

He performed a clumsy little pirouette to demonstrate his figure.

'Now, where were we?' he asked. 'Ah yes. *Mes aventures!* That's your actual French, you know.

'Well, I toddled off to do my little bit of research into human physical and emotional sensations and felt just awwwful! All alone and frightened for the first few days. And I'd never experienced so many sensations simultaneously. The sheer volume of sensory data you people receive and analyse during a single moment in time is just ridiculously overwhelming!

'You've got thousands of touchy-feely sensations both within and outside your bodies, from breezes on your cheeks to wind in your bellies. You've only got to move your head a centimetre and you're having to process new, subtle changes in a vast array of visual data. Your ears are bombarded by a thousand delicate or bawdy sounds over which you have precious little control at all. There's a constant shift in external and internal smells and tastes from farty-farty to rosy-Chanel, and from divinely delicious to pukey putrescence, so you're constantly trying to assimilate those into some kind of interpretation of the environment.

'And thoughts, thoughts, thoughts just keep popping up and deluging incessantly into and out of your consciousness... Do you know, I really do think that in those first few days after I arrived, I could have gone completely and totally insane? Do you realise, for example, that I can name at least thirty-five sensations I'm feeling now, just standing here? No! No! Tell a lie! Seventy-three!

'Let me elaborate. Ah, yes. One: the aftertaste of that food and there's at least twenty-three different tastes and textures in just those tiny canapés. Two: a slight numbing feeling in my upper right molar. Three: a tension in my medial pterygoid muscle. Four: the tiniest of pressure points on my—'

'Ian!' Dunstable interrupted sharply. 'Your party's going to be over soon.'

'Alright! Alright!' Vader replied irritably. 'I don't like you so much today, Gerald! You're not being at all nice to me.

'What was I saying?' he asked Ray.

'You were speaking of sensations,' the Companion replied.

It was apparent that Vader avoided all contact with the Companion.

'Thank you, "the boy"', he said to Ray. 'Well, I got an itchy back from one of those dreadful houses I stayed at. Fleas or some kind of human parasite, I think!'

He shuddered at the recollection.

'But, do you know, I would never have believed that scratching the right spot could be such sensual bliss!

'Anyway, what do you think happened then?' he asked dramatically.

His audience looked blankly at him. He seemed completely unhinged.

'No? Nobody guessing? Well, I'll tell you. I. Discovered. Cheese!'

He paused, anticipating an enthusiastic reception.

'Cheese, darlings!' he repeated, looking at each of them in turn and studying their faces for recognition of this extraordinary turning point in his life. The subsequent silence, as he awaited their appreciation, lengthened to embarrassing proportions.

'Thirty-four different varieties of cheese!' he finally clarified with exasperation. 'All in one shop! And every single one of them quite different on the palate! Quite extraordinary!

'Back at my squalid dwelling, I spent a dreadful hour trying all thirty-four of them. I managed to shove two of them into my mouth at a time! Of course, by the time I'd finished I was appallingly sick, but then who wouldn't be? Mind you, there's something rather marvellous about the relief you get from vomiting, if you've never experienced it before,' he added happily.

'Anyway, I was absolutely, totally, one hundred per cent hooked! I began to see the tremendous possibilities for sensual experimentation here and thought, *Go for it!* Now there's a phrase that Gerald uses a lot: "Go for it!" It means just do what you want for yourself but pretend it's dynamic and has a point to it.

'Well, I knew I didn't want to be lonely, frightened and living in horrid conditions, so I did some research about the wealthy, powerful people living here. You see, if you're wealthy and powerful, you have so much more control over your life, can indulge in all kinds of sensory pleasures and can manipulate all the silly little people around to serve your needs and do what you want.

'Of course, Gerald's name kept cropping up, didn't it? He's a very big fish in a very, very small pond, isn't he? I showed him some ideas about quantum processors and superconductors, that kind of stuff. Very primitive, really.

'He was a little sceptical at first, weren't you, Gerald? I'm just saying you were a little sceptical to begin with, Gerald.'

Dunstable looked up from his paperwork and smiled insincerely at Vader. The loony swine was really pushing his luck tonight! He could have cheerfully strangled him.

'Nice man,' Vader observed. 'Now, where was I? Oh, yes. Well, once that hopelessly incompetent moron, Stapleton, looked at it, we were off! Gerald's a positive whirlwind where money and power are involved, aren't you, Gerald? I mean, what else is there to do on this dump you call "Mother Earth"? Even the name sounds dull and mucky. Earth! Urrrgh!

'You do realise, don't you, that Gerald is the revered chair of Vader International and all these other charities and committees. A truly great, great man and philanthropist in the eyes of the community. Well, personally I think he's just in them to make himself feel powerful. So he doesn't feel so lonely, fearful and inadequate, probably.'

'Ian, will you please stop?!' Dunstable's tone of voice was sharp and impatient.

'Ooh! Have I dropped another social clanger there again? I'm awfully sorry, Gerald. Gerald's very intimidating when you cross him, isn't he?' he said to Ray with a sly smile.

'Anyway, Gerald got together all the finance and away we went! Do you know, he estimates we can make at least a hundred million "smackeroonies" in our second year of operation alone? Actually, it's probably ten times that amount because Gerald never tells me the truth. We pretend all the time, don't we, Gerald? He pretends he likes me, and I pretend to not understand what's really going on. As a partnership, and like many marriages and relationships here, it works perfectly really.'

'One of our most important directives was non-interference in the species' development and culture.' The Companion spoke forcibly.

'Oh God, isn't he a bore!' Vader sneered, raising his eyes to the ceiling. 'No, Mr Dreary-Pants! Our primary directive was to "*integrate*" into the primary species' culture. And I have done. Brilliantly!

'And, what's more, I have all the evidence to prove it. What I call "My Ten-Point Plan to Being Fashionably Human in the Age of Social Media". Very à la mode and contemporaneous!

'Numero one: I spend every minute I have indulging myself. Two: I'm enthusiastically positive about everything all the time, no matter how duff it actually is! Three: I don't examine, reflect on, or contemplate anything. Four: I pretend to be happy every moment of the day! Five: I aspire to be very "spiritual", and say how much I adore my fellow man, nature, clouds, poetry, doggies, kittens, theatre, fluffy things, et cetera, et cetera, et cetera!

'Six: I buy into and follow the very latest fads and fashions and always make sure I never stand out from the crowd. Seven: I'm a victim and take absolutely no responsibility at all for any of my own actions! Eight: I believe and follow everything the governing classes tell me. Nine: I just adore what you people have done to the concept of charity; keeping loads and loads of dosh for oneself whilst being able to patronise the losers with just the tiniest fraction of it; all to the accompaniment of such lovely, lovely slavish praise. And, finally and most importantly, ten: I never question a solitary thing!

'Now, Mr Droopy-Drawers,' he concluded to the Companion, 'if that isn't being in tune and on trend with everything on the western hemisphere of the third planet from the Sun, I really, really don't know what is!

'Do you know, when Gerald finally works out who I am and what my profile is, I'm going on Fakebook, and I'm going to spend all day going on and on about how great and crazy I am! And I'm joining Twatter, and I'm going to Twat people!'

'It's Facebook and Twitter, Ian! And you "Tweet", you don't "Twat"!' Dunstable corrected, frustrated with how regularly Vader got those wrong.

He suspected that Vader did it on purpose for attention, or to wind him up.

Vader continued as if he hadn't heard him. 'And, as I said, I'm going to do lots of things for charity so people will love and adore me. I mean, I really don't want to do anything for the actual people themselves, you understand. You know, abused women and children or the elderly or the sick, because that's just depressing and terribly, terribly hard work, isn't it!' he said, pursing his mouth in disgust.

'Do you realise that celebrities, élites and the really important people here can get away with behaving absolutely appallingly to the rest of the "scum", if they just front up a "charidy". Gerald's super in that respect! He's always in the paper representing some charity.

'To be honest, I don't really understand what charity means to some of you people, particularly Gerald here. I thought it meant that you actually did things for people who were less fortunate than yourself. But Gerald just turns up at charity dinners, balls and events or gives speeches. Gerald's on loads of charity committees and people say he's ever so wonderful. And he absolutely can't stand being around sick, unimportant, poor people or those with problems!'

'Ian, you really are going too far tonight!' Dunstable warned, the tone threatening.

Vader appeared not to hear again. 'So, after people think I'm generous and thoughtful I'm planning to go into politics. That's really brilliant because you can have all this power and influence and you don't have to believe in anything at all! "The Party" takes care of all that philosophical and ethical mumbo-jumbo for you. All you have to do is blindly follow whatever it says and spout general rubbish about how great this or that country *can* be again, and how proud you are of your fellow citizens. Provided they're doing exactly what you tell them, of course, and not being an arse, an obstacle or a nuisance!'

He was suddenly struck by a thought. 'Do you know, I've just realised why the Government doesn't just give all the money directly to the people and animals who need it. It's because of that income tax thingummy Gerald's so desperate to avoid paying.

'Gerald religiously believes that people shouldn't have to pay taxes. That they should jolly well work hard, look after themselves and not rely on the state or others for help. Jolly, jolly right, I say and particularly marvellous, counterintuitive thinking on Gerald's part because he's never produced an original thing, inherited all his wealth and hasn't done a hard day's manual labour in his entire life. Isn't that right, Gerald?'

'Ian, I think the party's gone on quite long enough—' Dunstable began.

'Gerald says the really, really, really best thing to be is the head of a big corporation or finance company. You see, you can control all the politicians, do all sorts of terrible things to people for your own gains, and nobody knows who you are. But I want to be loved by everybody, so that's why I'll probably become a politician.

'Anyway, while I'm building up my confidence, I live here all nice and cosy. Gerald treats me like a child and Margaret the old-cow-nurse takes care of my medications. And I've got my computer games and films and all these TV channels I never watch. And Margaret arranges the delivery of all these different foods and magazines about celebrities. And I can eat what I like and, who knows, I may even have a go at... er,' he lowered his voice, '"sex" with someone else.'

Vader moved across to the Companion. 'It's just a case then, of sorting this one out,' he pointed a thumb at him, 'so he doesn't spoil things for me.'

He lowered his voice to a loud whisper Dunstable would clearly hear. 'Gerald says *he's* going to deal with the Other. But to be perfectly honest, he can't. You see, he's nowhere near as clever or brave as he thinks and pretends to be. In fact, confidentially, between the three of us, I find him bland, rather thick and totally self-obsessed.'

'Ian, that's it! That's enough!' Dunstable stated, all patience gone. He rose from his chair and began to come around the side of the desk but stopped abruptly as Vader spoke.

'Oooh, I say! Look at this!' Vader exclaimed, happy surprise in his voice.

He had taken out an automatic pistol from his suit pocket, with a silencer attached to it, and held it out for them all to see, as a very young child might hold out a worm.

'Where… where did you get that from?' Dunstable asked, falteringly.

'It's a Glock, Gerald. A Glllllock,' Vader said, pulling back and releasing the slide mechanism as a bullet entered the chamber.

'A polymer-framed, short recoil-operated, locked-breech, semi-automatic pistol! And that's a silencer on the end there. Can you see? It keeps the racket down. I gave a pile of those fifty-pound notes you let me keep in my bedroom cabinet to one of Mr Manley's men and he got it for me. I got so good with the computer-game pistol I thought I'd have a go at the real thing.'

He pointed the gun in Dunstable's direction.

'What…what do you think you're doing—' Dunstable started to say.

The desk-light next to Dunstable suddenly shot off the table and a loud, tinny bang echoed around the room. There was smoke and a smell of cordite. Dunstable flinched, his eyes widening in panic.

Vader turned the muzzle of the silencer towards his mouth and blew away the smoke, as an old film-cowboy might. He pulled back the slide mechanism and the shell-case ejected tinklingly onto the marble-tiled floor as he pointed the gun again at Dunstable.

'Considering that's the first time I've fired it, that was really rather good, wasn't it? It's got much more of a kick to it than the computer-game gun, but I think I'm probably the rootingest, tootingest, best durned gunfighter – Oh, I can't remember all the other silly words, but I do love that cowboy-video game and all those classic Western films, don't you?' he asked Ray.

Ray's mouth was wide-open.

'I want to talk, Gerald, and you aren't letting me!' Vader added petulantly and then smiled in his bright, menacing way, 'I tell you what, Gerald. If you interrupt me one more time, I'm going to feel totally justified blowing your brains all over the walls.'

Dunstable was trembling. The sick, little maniac might do anything, he thought desperately. He forced himself to breathe slowly and become calm.

'Ian,' he said, in his most soothing voice which had never failed to modify Vader's erratic behaviour in the past, 'Ian, don't you think a couple of pills and a bit of a lie-down would do you—'

One of the computer monitors, next to where the light had been, somersaulted off the desk with a spraying of glass-splinters hitting the wall behind. Dunstable looked down at the monitor lying on the floor and saw a neat, smoking hole in the back of it. His chin began to twitch, and his complexion became sweaty and ashen.

'My! You look a little icky, Gerald, doesn't he?' Vader appealed to the others, 'Perhaps *you* should have a little lie-down and then, when I've finished, you can be my very, very, very, very, very, very, very, very, very, very, very, very bestest friend ever again. Come over here and sit down. There's a good Gerald,' he concluded in a tone that brooked no argument.

Dazed, Dunstable moved from beside the desk and slowly lowered himself into the chair indicated. A charged silence lay on the room. Leary and Ray had involuntarily leapt up from their seats after the first shot and stood apparently paralysed. Ray was aware of increasing saliva in his mouth and a powerful urge to throw up. Only the Companion had remained where he was, studying Vader's every move with intense concentration.

'Well, come on! Everybody sit down again! Good! And what shall we do now?' Vader asked, as if he were a child hosting his own birthday party.

'Look… look,' Leary began, leaning forward in his chair, 'I don't know what's going on here, pal, but I got to get this lad home, see? I'll come back later.'

'Honest?' Vader asked guilelessly.

'Yeah, honest, pal. I give me word.'

'And we all know the value of *your* word, don't we, Garrrry?' Vader's smile was demonic as he spoke. 'My oh my! You're about as trustworthy as a rattlesnake sitting on a cactus spine, partner. But… well, I'm afraid things have moved on and just aren't quite that simple anymore, Garry.'

'What do you mean?'

'Well, for example, I can hardly let young "the boy" here go wandering around blabbing all about me, can I?'

'Well, what are you going to do?' Leary asked.

'Well, I don't know,' Vader replied, looking around the room as if searching for inspiration.

He stopped and smiled broadly. 'I know! I could shoot him!'

He shrugged. Ray looked across at his uncle, terrified.

'You what?' Leary asked, paling.

'I said, "I could shoot him". "Kill" sounds so brutal and final, doesn't it? Alright. Let's use one of your better euphemisms for murder. I could "eliminate him". "Terminate him". "Despatch him". "Take him out". Ooh no! That sounds a bit like a high-school date, doesn't it?'

He giggled and then looked at the group, angered by their horrified expressions.

'Well, don't all look at me like that! I didn't say I wanted to kill him.' He paused. 'Mind you, I've never killed anyone before. I mean, I might find I quite like it. I mean, if you look at your history, lots and lots of your species appear to enjoy killing.

'I mean, come on, let's face it, you lot have shot, stabbed, skewered, mangled, burnt, bombed, ripped, beaten, battered, throttled, torn, suffocated and strangled literally millions! Why, just the other day I was playing this incredibly popular video game where you're a gangster and you go around killing or torturing all these—'

'Ian!' Dunstable exclaimed, appalled at the turn events were taking. 'We don't just "murder" people like that here!'

'Ohhh, Gerald! Not you as well! Now you know, as well as I do, that a considerable amount of our finance for research comes from military sources, who happen to be very interested in different ways of "topping" people. Don't go all silly and soft on me now. Plllease!'

The Companion raised himself painfully to his feet. 'I have heard enough. We must leave. Now.'

He made to move towards Vader who pointed the gun at his head.

'If you come any closer, I shall certainly use this on you. I really have no desire to, but I will.'

'For God's sake, Ian!' Dunstable shouted, standing up.

'For whose sake?' questioned Vader. 'You really are disappointing me today, Gerald. I've never seen any evidence at all that you believe in a creator. I thought this God and Christianity stuff was supposed to be about being aware of a greater, more magnanimous power in the universe, and loving everybody.

'I know you're a lay preacher in your church and that makes you look all caring and kind and everything, but you actually despise poor people and drug addicts and "scroungers" as you call them. In fact, you avoid them as much as possible. As for the "God" bit; what on earth is that supposed to be about?'

He shook his head despairingly. 'You so don't know who you are, Gerald. You don't even realise you're gay. Now, be a good boy and sit down and shut up. In fact, all of you settle back down. Let's all be comfortable. I'll just keep standing and being the most important one here.'

He turned his attention back to Ray. 'Tell me, Raymond. It is Raymond, isn't it? I thought the use of your Christian name might... kind of... establish a more... Well, a more personal, intimate, comforting kind of relationship between us now that I'm planning to despatch you to oblivion.

'So, tell me, Raymond, and this isn't just idle curiosity. Well, actually, it is really. But just tell me. Now that I am planning to "murder you", how do you feel at this precise moment?'

Ray's lower face muscles were twitching.

'Really, dear boy,' Vader said, sounding genuinely kind, 'all this,' and he indicated the room and the view out to sea, 'all this,' he repeated, and the smile left his face and he looked momentarily devastated, 'it's… nothing. Absolutely nothing. It's the sensations of a moment. Gone forever. Pffft!'

He clicked his fingers.

Leary placed himself in front of Ray. 'You're not touching him, Vader!'

He pointed a shaking finger at him, which made Vader guffaw delightedly.

'Heroism! Golly gosh! I've never seen that here before! How wonderful! But rather scary I would imagine! Oh, yes. I can see by your wobbly hand that it is.'

'Shut your mouth, you bloody freak!' Leary shouted.

'Golly! Golly! Golly!' Vader said. 'This is just getting better and better! Am I meant to feel angry now? Yes. Yes. I really do believe I can feel… just a little smidgen of anger. Do, please, continue, Garry. This is absolutely riveting!'

'Listen!' Leary said, his voice breaking as he spoke. 'I'm not interested in your sick games. You'll touch this boy over my dead body.'

'Through it, I would imagine, unless you move a little more to the right,' Vader replied calmly, indicating the pistol. 'Do you know, Garry, I find your whole behaviour riddled with inconsistencies. I mean "the boy" here, as you call him, seems like quite a decent little chap but he doesn't look very happy most of the time, does he? Not a happy chappie at all. You could argue that I'd be sort of doing the little blighter a favour really, couldn't you? Putting him out of his misery, so to speak.

'I mean, you people here are always pretending that everyone's of equal value and gets treated the same. And then some famous, idiot actor, musician, politician, royal, sportsman drops dead, and everybody's saying what a terribly sad tragedy it is. Yet they couldn't give a damn about some old dear around the corner, who's popped her clogs in a care home!

'I mean, "the boy" here, he's hardly important, is he? Honestly. No money! No status! Not famous! Not in Gerald's league at all! Honestly and truthfully, what possible loss to the world is he likely to represent, if he "shuffles off this mortal coil" a little prematurely?

'You're just so, so all over the place, Garry. You quite cheerfully betray my colleagues and "the boy" himself. Then, you get all confused and sentimental when I take the basic proposition you act on, "Looking After Number One", to its full and logical conclusion. Killing the little fellow here. Well, it just simplifies things for me, doesn't it?'

He continued, his face frowning. 'I mean, I'm sure your display of concern is all very... What's the term? Oh, yes. "Noble". Personally, I find it rather tragic and pathetic. As Gerald always says, "Go for it!" Being human is just about satisfying one's desires, isn't it?'

He paused. 'Still, I expect that's what you're doing now, isn't it? Trying to regain the boy's respect and affection, I mean. Do you know, I find that awfully, awfully sweet!'

'Do something!' Leary shouted at the Companion.

'Oh, him!' Vader remarked, tutting. 'You'll find him very disappointing. All moral rectitude and stuffed shirt, but very little in the way of action.'

At that moment the sound of the lift moving could be heard.

'Oh dear,' Vader sighed. 'Now who's this?'

As he moved towards the lift the Companion suddenly threw himself at him, knocking him off balance to the floor. As Vader fell, the pistol fired, and the Companion jerked violently backwards.

Leary leapt onto Vader as he hit the floor.

'Get out of here!' he shouted to Ray, as he delivered a flurry of furious punches at Vader.

But Ray moved forward to help, receiving a kick from Vader's flailing legs that knocked him back over one of the easy chairs. To a shocked Ray the struggle looked nothing like the carefully choreographed, fast-edited fights he'd seen at the cinema but a vicious, animalistic, savage free-for-all. Vader used every physical tactic at his disposal, punching, scratching, gouging, biting and finally kicking his way out of the mêlée. Crawling away quickly on all fours, he stood up unsteadily by the lift doors.

His thick, blond hair, a wig, had detached from the left-hand side of his head. It hung upside down over his right ear, revealing a completely white, bald skull which contrasted, to ridiculous effect, with the line of orange fake tan covering the rest of his head. His nose was bleeding and there were red marks around his right eye and scratches on his chin. His collar was torn, and his tie pulled tight around the side of his neck. The breast pocket of his silk suit was ripped and hanging.

He was sobbing hysterically, his body juddering with hurt, shock and outrage. The gun was still in his hand, shaking dangerously. The Companion lay slumped, bleeding, against the base of the sofa. Leary, his face bloody with cuts and scratches, pulled himself up groggily, using one of the chairs for support. Vader had kicked him in the side of the head, and he'd passed out briefly.

Vader's body shuddered with heaving sobs as he screamed out his words, spit flying across the room. 'That really, really hurt me!'

Suddenly, he caught sight of his torn and distressed appearance in the mirror wall. He looked disbelievingly at his reflection.

'Look at me!' he screamed, his sentences broken up by his heaving sobs. 'Just look at me! You've gone and spoilt everything! I looked really, really handsome and trendy and now... Now. Now, I look stupid! And... and you! You've spoilt my party!

'I haven't had any proper friends. And... and you. You were... you were all going to be my friends. And... and now you've spoilt it all!'

Vader surrendered himself to his sobs. Leary, stumbling slightly as he shook his head to clear it, knocked a glass off the arm of a chair. As it shattered, Vader came out of his sobbing fit and calmed with ice-cold fury. He pointed the gun at Leary, gripping it with both hands to steady it.

'I didn't do anything to you at all!' he screamed. 'Well, now you're going to get it back! Twice as hard!'

Leary, swaying slightly, positioned himself so that he was completely covering Ray stood behind him.

'Listen, Ray,' he muttered, like a bad ventriloquist, turning his head slightly toward him, 'edge away from me. The second he shoots, you run for that fire-escape door, and don't look back. Right?'

Then he took three steps toward Vader, who flinched.

Isn't it supposed to be harder for a man to kill someone when they're close enough to be able to see the colour of their eyes and smell them? he thought.

They were less than a couple of metres apart, and Leary looked intently in Vader's face, strangely calm and accepting of his fate. Vader stood wavering. Then he slowly and deliberately pulled back the hammer of the automatic and sighted the muzzle at the centre of Leary's forehead.

Ohhhh, shit, Leary recognised, with a mental shrug of resignation. *But then, this is no man, though, is it?*

He closed his eyes. There was a loud ping, the lift doors opened and there stood what remained of Zita Truman.

THIRTY-EIGHT

'You and Spencer will have as much information as I have on this Derringham farce and you're leading the investigation. You'd better be on top form because it's a damned awful mess!' Phillip Faulkner concluded.

Windridge nodded, feeling pretty well exhausted. It was a quarter to midnight and today's shift had started at 7.00am. Just on the point of leaving for home the section head, Greenhawn, had disdainfully dropped a note on the desk, informing of an immediate meeting with the director.

'Any problems you foresee working with Spencer?' Faulkner asked.

'Well, he's not exactly my cup of tea,' Windridge replied.

That was an understatement; couldn't stand him!

'Yes, well I'm not running a dating agency, am I? Can you work with the man or not?'

'Of course.'

Windridge watched the director reach for his tablets and recognised the wisdom of refraining from any further criticism of Spencer, who was a young, ambitious, highly effective, sycophantic-to-superiors, arrogant, nasty piece of work.

'Get yourself issued with the usual field equipment.' The director paused. 'How long since you used one in anger?'

'Seventeen months, twenty-three—' Windridge began.

'Fine. Fine,' Faulkner interrupted. 'Need any practice?'

'The last armourer said I could practise until I retired, but he still couldn't guarantee I'd win a fluffy toy at the fairground. His words. They're not really my style, sir.'

'Perhaps, if they had been your style—' The director stopped himself, feeling awkward. 'Look, you probably won't need to employ one on a case of this sort anyway. I'm giving you a real opportunity here, you know...' the director continued, looking anywhere but into Windridge's eyes. 'Well, it's a real opportunity to conclude your career with dignity restored.'

'I do recognise and appreciate that, sir,' Windridge replied sincerely.

The director always looked uncomfortable when he alluded to the 'Zhang' case. Guilt? Shame? Disgust? Who knew?

'Right. Clear your desk of any cases you're engaged in. I've told Greenhawn you're off his team.'

'That must have been upsetting for him,' Windridge observed with a straight face.

Greenhawn would be busily organising one of his excruciatingly awful staff socials to celebrate the departure.

'Tell me, do you actually get on with any of your colleagues?' Faulkner asked wearily.

'Just the non-fakes.'

'Yes… Well, you probably don't have a wide circle of friends here, then. You didn't exactly pick the right profession if you were looking for twenty-four-hour authenticity, did you?'

'No. I was misinformed at the time.'

The director hunched forward in his chair angrily and looked directly into his subordinate's eyes. 'Listen, Windridge, James Maitland and I are putting ourselves on the line with regards to this, so I don't particularly appreciate smart aleck comments. Right? You've got some very distinct strikes against you already. Age and the other things we pretend aren't issues here. So, don't let either of us down.'

'I won't, sir.'

Back home, Windridge began to process the incredible information just delivered by Faulkner. The existence of alien life, clearly far advanced from our own species, had finally been confirmed. We were not alone in the universe.

This was the most culturally, mind-blowingly astounding event in the whole of human history, and Faulkner had just reduced its amazing significance into a basic management problem. The same rules were to apply to this case as with every other. Keep the general populace as ignorant as possible, for 'they' were considered just too unstable to be able to handle such information without careful supervision and top-down guidance.

That might have been understandable if the 'people at the top' actually knew what they were doing. But Windridge knew, from bitter experience, that they really hadn't got much more of a clue than the average citizen they constantly patronised. They screwed things up just as thoroughly and spectacularly as any incompetent plumber, builder, fast-food operative or dust-cart worker! The only difference was their capacity to cover over their mistakes. A leaking tap, leaning wall, inedible dish and unemptied bin were all glaring evidence of the working class's incompetence.

In the higher world of the 'professional classes' it was very, very difficult to pinpoint incompetence. Reams and reams of written evidence would have to be ploughed through – boring, arcane and confusing. Then you had only to instigate a 'public inquiry' to guarantee sufficient sand blown into the electorate's eyes, one victim scapegoated and nobody of significance 'hung out to dry'. For, in such circumstances there was an unspoken conspiracy that 'We' all stuck together.

Let the average citizen get a peek into what really went on 'at the top' and respect would vanish, and revolution probably follow.

Back in Whitehall, Faulkner stood up, stretching himself in a futile attempt to achieve some sense of wellbeing. Was he losing his touch finally? Becoming sentimental in his old age? Windridge was a definite one-off in the service; a hand-me-down from Maitland, who rated them highly. Windridge had better do this right! The usual 'early-retirement-knighthood-for-an-official-cock-up', awaited the director if his current, disastrous run of luck continued. Windridge faced a lot worse than that if this affair got further screwed up.

Well, he concluded, *that was one way of guaranteeing Windridge's total devotion, loyalty and motivation in the game ahead.*

THIRTY-NINE

Leary opened his eyes. There was no hole in his forehead, and that 'ping' sound had been the lift announcing its arrival. Zita Truman stood in its entrance, her clothing gone and little of the original, artificial flesh covering her body remaining. The exposed metal was dented, scraped and scratched on the chest, back and upper thighs. Electrical sparking came from the end of her left wrist where the hand should have been. The left arm occasionally jerked at the shoulder.

The front of the face was pitted with holes, but most of the flesh features remained. The flap of skin over the forehead had been torn off down the side of the face to the jawline, in a triangular shape that tapered to a point. Water dripped down her. Warrington, looking dazed, was standing behind. She stepped awkwardly into the room; her right leg seemed also to be malfunctioning.

'Companion,' she said, and the voice had lost any trace of softness to it. It was metallic, hard and slightly slow, like an old, wind-up gramophone player, running out of power. She stood some moments surveying the room.

Vader's sobbing ceased, for his eyes were transfixed on Truman and terror-stricken. The gun was now pointing unsteadily at her. Truman, ignoring him, moved clumsily across to the Companion, her right leg dragging. She gently lifted him onto the sofa and dressed his wounds with linen napkins from the table.

She looked across at Ray as if seeking his help. Ray moved and, not knowing what else to do, took hold of the Companion's hand. The Companion opened his eyes and gave a gentle, grateful smile. Truman hobbled across to Vader.

'What have you done?' she demanded.

'It wasn't my fault! The gun went off! I didn't mean it. He... he attacked me!' Vader replied falteringly. 'It was your fault too! You... you were supposed to be taking care of me! And you... you just left me here! Abandoned me. Here! In this terrible, terrible, terrible place!'

'You knew how the Fusion process was to work,' Truman began. 'We discussed it in every briefing before we embarked on the mission. It absolutely depends on prolonged separation from each other. Processing in isolation the incoming data and sensations is the most fertile and challenging element of the Fusion exercise.'

'Listen to yourself! Just listen! "Processing incoming data"! You even talk like a machine, now! That's because you're locked up safe inside one! But who... who got the most traumatising element? Whose job was it to "process sensations"? Mine! Mine! I did it!

'Because you have no idea and never can have what emotions and sensations these Homo Sapiens suffer! How they survive even an hour in this world is little short of miraculous! You should have chosen a different planet! You should have chosen a better place! You should have protected us!' he challenged furiously.

'I admit that I did not anticipate, with sufficient rigour, the challenges this world presents – the horrors, the terrors, the pleasures. I did not fully appreciate the specific challenges that you might face. But you survived,' Truman continued, 'and the quality of experience you have received here may well result in the greatest Fusion yet.'

'I don't care about the stupid Fusion! Don't you understand that?! I don't care about some future, theoretical, stupid state-of-being! I want comfort now! I want it now! Please! Please!'

'We must leave. They cannot survive without the Fusion.' Truman pointed at the prone Companion. 'And there is further peril, for another creature is proceeding here. It is absolutely imperative that we leave. Now.'

'No! No! I'm not going! You and him!' Vader indicated the Companion. 'You don't understand! I had no idea what fear, loneliness or death were until you made us come here.

'I know now!' he screeched. 'I've been terrified every minute I've been here. Here, inside this ridiculously vulnerable, soft body. They're so easily damaged! The threat of death or pain or wounding is with them every single second of their lives. They're surrounded by danger and death!

'There are earthquakes, volcanoes, hurricanes, tsunamis and forest fires! And there's disease and famine and violence and war and accidents and ignorance! Do you realise? Do you get it? They never get to know each other! They are born alone! *And they die alone!*

'I know that terror now! I can feel that loneliness. I can feel that closeness to death with every breath I take! So, I'm not going anywhere! I'm staying right here in this room! Here, where it's warm, cosy, safe and I can distract my mind every second of the day!'

'We must fuse, or the mission here will have been for nothing.'

'I don't care about the stupid, stupid mission! I'm frightened! Can you understand that? Really understand that?'

Vader started to sob again, his voice broken by his gulps for air. 'What happens if the Fusion goes wrong? And it can! You know it can! We should never have come here! You made us, and we should never have come!'

'What of our companion?' Truman asked, pointing at the sick and bleeding figure.

'Who gives a damn! Tough if he dies before me! Better if he dies before me! I'm never going to believe I can die! That's the credo I've learnt here!'

He began rubbing his hands together desperately as if washing them. He suddenly put them to his face and drew their smell deeply into his lungs.

'Oh, no! No, I can still smell the decay! I can smell the death! There is no escape!'

He looked around desperately for help and saw Ray comforting his companion. Throwing the gun across the room, he ran and fell on his knees before the startled lad.

'Help me!' he begged him. 'Please, please, please help me!'

Ray, shocked, looked down at the pathetic, clownish figure with the cuts, blood, ridiculous wig and tan; red, tear-filled eyes, running, bloody nose and the look of absolute terror and confusion on its face.

And suddenly, he wasn't looking at a man/alien anymore. He was looking at a lost, totally open and utterly vulnerable soul who could have been any age.

Oddly, Ray didn't feel any anger or resentment for the terror the begging figure had made him endure just minutes before. He understood that this creature was simply terrified by life. Confused and terrified by it. As Ray, himself, so often had been. And probably always would be. The difference was that the kneeling figure expressed it so publicly. And so, so nakedly!

Because Vader, at that moment, wasn't trying to drink, bluff or joke himself out of the uncertainty and pain of living and dying as Garry did. Or brutalise himself out of it as Manley did. Or 'ego' himself out of it as Dunstable did. Or simply distract himself from it as Ray so often did.

He was just facing it and being what he was. Ray, tentatively reaching out his hand, gently touched the white, bald top of the head and found himself murmuring softly, 'You'll be okay. Really. You'll be okay...'

And for Truman, looking at the abandoned, forlorn figure surrendering himself so completely to his grief, and the young human comforting him, suddenly, something clicked. Clicked into place. She had finally begun to comprehend the vastness of Vader's raw, visceral pain. She really hadn't understood until this moment what he had borne. His vulnerability, absurdity, pomposity, grief, madness and fear in the face of so many unknown terrors had repelled before. But now they touched her. She limped slowly across to him.

'I am truly, truly sorry for what you have suffered. I had no idea. Please... please will you forgive me?'

Vader, looking up at the battered, crippled mechanism, began to sense what traumas the creature inside also had undergone. Vicious, murderous forces had been unleashed upon her. Beings had deprecated, despised, feared and hated her enough to want to extinguish and obliterate her whole existence.

The fact that she had asked his forgiveness signified so much to him at that moment. It meant that she had recognised his pain and distress, the indignities he had suffered, the bizarre behaviours he had adopted to cope, and had regretted her role in them.

She had recognised that she had abandoned him and fouled things up, not out of cruel intent, but through ignorance and... incompetence. She had had no concept of just how much both colleagues would have to endure here. Her simple recognition seemed to answer so many of the injustices Vader had had to bear. Someone just recognising the pain, affording the respect for it, and trying to make amends for it. That was strangely... enough.

Ray moved aside as Truman gently stroked Vader's head. At the touch, his body seemed to relax, his sobs gradually subsiding. He felt... not so alone anymore. Resting his forehead gently on the Companion's chest, he reached out his hand to the Companion's, held, then stroked and kissed it.

Leary, looking at his nephew and the three figures, was surprised to find himself suddenly feeling emotional. The scene reminded him of how his mum had stroked his face when she was in the final stages of cancer in the hospital bed, all those years ago. Just caressed it gently with those soft, almost translucent white hands, while she looked steadily into his eyes, and he'd seen and knew the love there for him.

He hadn't cried once since that day! Not once in twenty-seven years! Not since Mum had died when he was just fifteen and Ray's dad was nine and his own father had told them that feeling sorry for themselves was a luxury none of them could afford. That they were all going to have to just 'buck up and get on with it'.

And he wasn't going to start that kind of stuff now, Leary decided, pushing his knuckles into his eyes, and wiping them as if he was just tired. He looked about the room surreptitiously to check that no one had seen him. And no one had.

His secret was safe.

FORTY

'Are you ready?' Truman asked.

Vader nodded and the Companion gently squeezed his hand to indicate his willingness.

Truman moved over to the recumbent figure of the Companion and lifted him as gently as she could. The Companion groaned quietly, involuntarily, as if he didn't wish to disturb anyone. Truman held him upright with her hand just under his armpit.

Vader slowly stood up, pulling off the wig and letting it fall to the floor. He dabbed his face gently with a napkin, looked at Ray and then smiled bashfully at him. It was a smile of recognition and warmth; of two beings meeting as intimate equals.

He nodded, then moved and took up a position opposite Truman and at an angle to the Companion, so that the three of them were like the points of a triangle if viewed from above.

'You will, please, move back,' Truman said to the others in the room. 'None of us is certain what will occur.

We would never have attempted this procedure before we had returned to our craft, but one of us is too close to non-existence to risk the delay.'

Then she slowly closed her eyes and opened up her mouth. The Companion and Vader assumed the same position.

Nothing happened for a minute or more and then, very slowly, so slowly that it was barely perceptible, fluorescent smoke or mist – turquoise blue from Truman, sunny yellow from the Companion and scarlet red from Vader – began to flow out of each mouth. There were sparks of light amongst it.

The mist flowed out at a level with their chests and remained there for what seemed like minutes. Ray, fascinated, seemed to have forgotten how to breathe. He took in a gulp of air like a pearl diver, but as quietly as he could, not wishing to break the spell of the moment.

The bodies on either side of Truman slowly sagged and pirouetted gently to the ground in awkward positions against her legs. Her mouth suddenly gaped as if the hinge of the jaw had broken. The lower jaw stayed put while the upper one moved backwards with the rest of her head. The mouth gaped ever wider, then ceased moving.

The three clouds of mist and sparks had remained separate, floating freely. They suddenly started to pulsate and then began to extend into tendrils that circled and weaved and whirled amongst themselves. The weaving motion increased in speed and intensity, suddenly illuminated with blue, red and yellow flashes of intense light, so that the room lit up as if a multi-coloured thunderstorm was occurring in it. There was a smell of ozone and sweetness in the air.

Ray sensed his uncle move beside him and felt compelled to shut his eyes, so searing was the brightness of the scene occurring. He could feel a warmth in the room, and it was soft and comforting, but the flashes of lightning he could still distinguish, even behind his closed lids, were starting to make him afraid.

The flashes appeared to diminish in intensity and, as Ray cautiously opened his eyes, the 'smoke' was beginning to change ever so slightly but then more rapidly into a clear, oval-shaped jelly with a halo of blue, yellow and red lights shimmering about its surface. It began to form in the centre of what had been the triangle and to pulsate.

Then, very slowly, it rose and glided towards Truman's gaping mouth. It seemed to falter momentarily, as if unwilling to enter, but then it gradually wriggled itself into the open maw and down the gullet.

Truman remained motionless while the top of the head began to move downward until finally the jaws closed together again. She stayed a matter of a minute unmoving. Then, the eyes gradually opened.

'Jeez!' Leary murmured. 'And for my next piggin' trick...'

Ray smiled. His uncle would always have to make a 'crack' to put life into some kind of perspective for himself; to reduce it to a size he could cope with. It sometimes spoilt the delicate mood of a moment, but that was who he was.

And that was okay.

FORTY-ONE

'Sorry,' Leary added quietly, 'I let you down bad, Ray, and I'm sorry.'

Ray felt an intense shiver of pleasure suddenly pass up his spine – his uncle calling him 'Ray' twice and apologising! How extraordinary was that!

'That's okay, Garry,' Ray murmured. 'Thanks for saying it. It means a lot.'

'*Uncle* Garry,' Leary corrected, a little peeved.

'Whatever rings your bell,' Ray answered quietly.

Leary took a sidelong look at his nephew. He was definitely changing, he thought, and he wasn't too sure if he altogether liked it.

Truman spoke and her voice, though still metallic, carried notes of warmth to it. 'The process has worked. We are complete. Our mission is almost accomplished.'

'What happened?' Ray asked.

'We have undergone Fusion. On the planet from which we originate,' Truman began.

'Oh, jeez,' Leary muttered to himself, rolling his eyes.

'Another bleedin' lecture.'

'All of us are born as three distinct entities. What you might simplistically call the intellectual, the emotional and the spiritual. We possess a common DNA and identity; possess some elements of the three but are separate and incomplete. We live our early years within proximity of each other.

'Biologically, we are at a very similar stage to you, Raymond. Most decide that living as three distinct beings is sufficient. That there is companionship and support always there. Some of us, and we three are such, long for a closer and more complete union. We can put ourselves forward as candidates for Fusion.'

'I'm sorry,' Ray said, 'but I still don't understand. What's "Fusion"?'

'The process that unites the three beings into one. It must be undertaken in challenging and hazardous conditions. That is why we travel to other planets with life on them and attempt to understand, empathise and integrate ourselves with the most predominant and advanced species there.

'No one has ever visited this world before. We have been overwhelmed by the challenges, complexities and sheer loneliness of the lives your species lead. You are such a contradiction, both magnificent and absurd at the same time. Your potential, however, is quite miraculous.

'We saw that potential in every human creature we encountered. But we also saw ego, ignorance, blame, selfishness, guilt and intolerance. We saw that powerful men like you, Gerald, dismiss so many of your fellow creatures as irrelevances and failures, and yet have no insight at all into why that should be the case. Indeed, you mask and aggressively defend your ignorance with a keen sense of contempt for common humanity.

'You refuse to recognise that you were born privileged whilst they were born deprived. That you now possess power whilst they are impotent. You have not earned these privileges, Gerald. Random circumstances allotted you them. You seem only interested in how your fellow beings can be manipulated to satisfy the needs of your ego. You do not know your neighbours, Gerald. You do not know yourself. And yet you have so much you can offer.'

Dunstable looked confused and annoyed. He was being patronised and demeaned at the same time, he thought.

'The most dangerous part of our mission is behind us, but we have still to travel some distance to our craft on the seabed, and this machine,' she indicated the robot body, 'has seen "better days" as you say here.'

She turned first to Leary. 'Goodbye, Mr Leary. Thank you for your assistance. It has been… an education.'

'Yeah,' Leary said. 'Look, I… I know I been a… a bit of a… Well, a bit of an arse, really.'

'Arse?' the Creature asked.

'Oh, jeez! Look, I know I ain't always acted right by you.'

'We have learnt so much from you, Mr Leary. You are a very brave and resourceful individual; a strangely compelling, paradoxical exemplar of all that is admirable… and… challenging about the human condition,' concluded the Creature, searching carefully for its words so as not to insult the human before it.

'Yeah, well I wouldn't know about that, see. Look, pal, you take care of yourself,' Leary said, winking. 'And don't come back too soon, eh?'

The Creature smiled. 'A witticism?' it asked.

'Yeah. Sort of,' Leary said, patting it on its upper arm.

It suddenly seemed to strike Dunstable that the Creature was leaving and never coming back.

'What am I supposed to do now?' he demanded.

'Gerald,' the Creature said, 'we leave you with all the technology we brought. We should not have given it, but it is too late to take it back. The processes will work. How you employ them is up to you now. Perhaps you could share the knowledge of them with your fellow species, so that all may benefit equally.'

Dunstable stood, looking increasingly suspicious and hostile at this thing that had been, partly, Ian Vader. Vader would never, ever have said such stuff! Sharing! Sharing equally! What it had just said amounted suspiciously to some type of damned communism!

'A word of advice, if you will accept it, Gerald,' the Creature continued. 'Look to Raymond. Look to your young people. They are honest and authentic. They are uncorrupted, they seldom pretend to be something they are not, and they have so much to offer if you will just give them the respect, patience and time they deserve and need.'

What the hell on earth had Gerald Dunstable, the foremost man in the county and son of Sir Robert and other illustrious ancestors, possibly got to learn from some common, ignorant little oik like Bradnock, who hadn't even begun shaving yet? Dunstable thought.

'You will find Mr Manley and his associates unconscious downstairs. There should be no long-term damage or side effects,' the Creature concluded.

Warrington had been standing in a state of total bewilderment. The Creature approached and Warrington leaned back, as if afraid he might be contaminated by some disease it carried.

'Thank you, Mr Warrington, for your assistance and honesty. You are a good human being.'

Finally, it stood before Ray and spoke quietly, so that no one else would overhear.

'We currently feel very, very, very confused and strange, Raymond. May we ask, what you are feeling?'

Ray stood a moment, startled. He realised that nobody had ever actually asked him that question before in his entire life!

'I… I don't know… If Mum and Dad ever find out about any of this, they'll kill me. No! No, I don't mean actually *kill* me. But ground me, or moan at me or something or other. But that's really not that bad, is it? 'Cos, I haven't done anything wrong anyway, have I?' Ray asked, surprised at this self-revelation.

'But how do you *feel,* Raymond?'

Ray shook his head, defeated. 'I can't really tell. Is… is that important?'

'Having survived our time here,' the Creature answered, 'it seems to us that the capacity to feel is probably the most important facility your species has on this planet. You possess minds of most remarkable sophistication with a power for rationalising, which is both impressive, but also very disturbing. It allows you to do terrible things to each other, but then justify them as "reasonable" or "progress". The people at the research station appeared to have excused their brutal treatment of us in the same manner.

'They seemed to know, in their very core of feeling, that such treatment of another living organism was wrong. But they rationalised and normalised it; for that seems to be what you tend to do here. They suppressed those feelings of pity, distress and concern in the interests of science, fame and the satisfaction of their own egos.

'When people behave like that here, the consequences are invariably harsh and cruel. Your history appears replete with such examples. It seems to us that suppressing natural feeling means that you lose touch with, and empathy for, people and the world in which you live. And then you lose insight and a sense of common humanity and purpose.

'That is why we believe "feeling" on this planet is so important. Indeed, we believe it is absolutely crucial for your future survival as a species. Once you remove empathy, life simply becomes a competition, with every creature fighting for itself. No civilisation in the universe has ever been built or sustained on that premise. Does this make sense?'

'Sort of. I think so.'

'So, Raymond, may we ask again, to increase our insight into human behaviour: how do you feel?'

'I... I feel okay, I suppose. That doesn't sound very spectacular really, does it? But it feels really big because I've never felt like this before. I... I don't feel such a weirdo and so alone somehow. Do you understand that?'

The Creature continued to look at him as if searching for further clarification.

'It's like,' Ray continued, stumbling for his words, 'it's like I've always felt bad because people have told me I was being "wet" or oversensitive, which I always thought was kind of feeble and pathetic. They've also told me I think too much.'

Ray paused and contemplated.

'But those can't be bad things, can they?' he asked uncertainly.

The Creature paused, thinking before continuing. 'No. No, Raymond, we do not see how thinking or feeling can be bad things. Surely being thoroughly aware of life around one can only be of benefit. However, it does seem rare, often inconvenient and mostly painful.'

The Creature paused. 'So, you feel "okay". May we ask? What does that feel like?'

'I've… I've just always felt bad about myself. Kind of like I didn't deserve to be here. Like I wasn't good enough somehow. I don't even know what for. But now. Well, it kind of feels like I've got a right to be here. Like I belong. Sorry, I'm not making much sense, am I?'

'It is good, feeling that you belong and have the right to exist?' the Creature asked.

'Well, it's probably the best you can hope for, isn't it?' Ray answered.

The Creature leaned in towards Ray, held his right hand and whispered, 'Do not leave the management of this world to the Dunstables. Trust yourself. Trust your feelings, your intuitions and communicate them. You have so, so much to give… Thank you.'

It pulled back, withdrew its hand and Ray felt something substantial left in his palm.

The Creature reached under its rib cage and withdrew two metal shrouds, the same type as the one it had used at Derringham. They unfurled and it placed each of the bodies in its own bag. The bags sealed themselves and the Creature hoisted them, one on each shoulder and walked slowly into the open lift.

It turned and stood there, looking out at them for a moment. Then the doors closed, and the lift descended.

FORTY-TWO

Actually, witnessing Vader leave hit Dunstable hard. He stumbled across to the desk and sat, his head deep in his hands.

All his brilliant planning wasted!

He couldn't even begin to figure where to start sorting out this monumental mess! Would the authorities trace the Creature back to him? What would happen to Vader International now that its founder had gone, and there was still so much to be done? What was he going to do about Manley? How was he going to go on with Leary, Warrington and the boy now they knew all his secrets? And then… And then…

The question that had been in the back of his mind for the last ten minutes and had suddenly popped to the front and wouldn't go away.

What exactly had Vader meant when he'd said that he, Gerald Dunstable, Christian, upright, leading light of Brookdale-on-Sea and all-round respected citizen, didn't realise he was *gay*?

'What was all that about?' Leary asked his nephew.

Ray stood a moment, frowning. 'Feeling okay about yourself, I think,' he said finally.

'What?' Leary asked, puzzled.

'I don't really understand it all, but I think they were telling me I'm okay. That there's nothing the matter with me,' Ray explained.

'Cheeky bloody get! 'Course there's nothing the matter with you! Bit wet now and then, but a good lad for all that.'

'You've never said anything like that to me before.'

'Yeah, well, don't go all soft on me yet, son. I ain't exactly been Mahatmacane Gandhi, have I? Mind, I'd have taken a bullet for you. Thought I was a definite goner there… That says something, don't it? Don't know if that's 'cos your life's worth it, or mine ain't.

'This has been the weirdest, bloody thing ever, Ray. I mean, when you come to look at it, I ain't really done that much, have I? Just found a bloke and then drove him here, really. But them diamonds! Man, them diamonds is going to make a real… Jesus!'

Leary's eyes looked blankly at the far wall.

'Here, Warrington!' he called across the room, looking alarmed. 'Truman give you them diamonds, didn't she? When you was in reception with her. She give you them, didn't she?'

'What? What you talking about, Leary? She had seven of them down there against her. I don't know what she did, but they all went down like sacks of spuds. Looked like some kind of taser type—'

'Yeah! Yeah! But she give you the stones, didn't she? Afterwards?' Leary insisted.

'No. She gave them you, didn't she? Look, if this is another of your bloody wind-ups, Leary...' Warrington began, but then recognised the sincere look of shock on the other man's face.

'I ain't bleedin' got 'em, Warrington! Oh, jeez!' Leary exclaimed, his eyes wide with horror. 'No! No! She can't have. She's still got the faffin' things with her!'

Both men rushed across to the office window and looked downwards to see the Creature, having crossed the railway line, slowly striding across the sand and shale steadily out to sea. The tide was out, but not far. Leary hammered the window but knew that he couldn't possibly be heard at that distance.

'Jeez! Oh, jeez!' he shouted.

He ran to the lift doors, Warrington close behind him.

'Christ! The lift's on the ground floor! Use the stairs!' Leary shouted.

Ray could hear them clattering down the stairwell. He stole a look to check that Dunstable was still slumped at the desk, then wandered over to the window where he opened his fist to find two packages.

One was bigger than the other and seemed to be holding a lot of little gemstones. He put them in his pocket to be looked at later. The other seemed to contain just one. He opened it and dropped the contents into the open palm of his right hand.

A diamond, the size of a quail's egg, lay there sparkling under the inset spotlights in the ceiling.

It looked magnificent!

Looking down through the window, Ray could see his uncle and Warrington running and shouting at each other as they clambered over the railway fencing that separated them from the shoreline. He couldn't see the Creature anymore.

He flicked the diamond into the air with his thumb. At its zenith, it hung there a split second, with the night stars behind it, before it fell back into his cupped palm with a satisfying slap sound.

Must be worth an absolute fortune, thought Ray. *Uncle Garry* will *be pleased.*

When Ray decided to get around to telling him.

ABOUT THE AUTHOR

The author was a teacher in the state secondary sector for many years and developed an abiding interest in the challenges facing people as they grow up and participate in societies. *The Truman Quest* was written to playfully celebrate the human need to identify with fellow creatures. He believes that, however crazy and egotistical Homo Sapiens as a species may present itself, on an individual level its potential for integrity and magnanimity is phenomenal.